Teagan

The Eight Book Three

By

Sharilyn Skye

Copyright 2020 by Sharilyn Skye

All Rights Reserved

Paperback ISBN: 9781733313476

First Edition: April 11th, 2020

Revision February 2021

Cover Design: PaigeLCroPhotography

Cover Photo: Dreamstime:© Branislav Ostojic

Dark Horse Publishing

Morgantown, WV

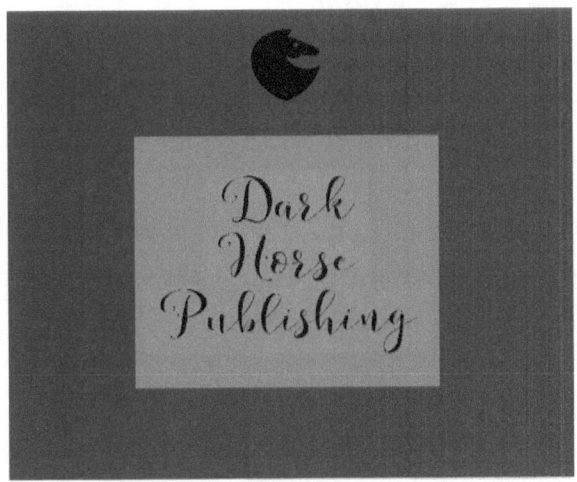

#countryroads

"But I've never ever been a calm blue sea

I have always been a storm."

~Stevie Nicks

"Hell is empty, and all the devils are here."

~William Shakespeare, The Tempest

"We may encounter many defeats, but we must not be defeated."

~ Maya Angelou

Chapter One

Teagan

Being kidnapped by trolls isn't what I thought it would be, not that I had put much thought into it. I never dreamed such a thing could happen. One minute I'm sitting with the rest of The Eight in Ari's bakery, and the next, I'm tossed over the shoulder of the giant, green, foul-smelling creature and taken rather gently through the countryside at a high rate of speed.

I heard the screams and clash of swords as I was carried away but could do nothing to stop it. Despite my bulk and strength, the beast holding me pinned me with one hand and hauled me across the land to this strange place.

I've been treated well so far. The Troll dropped me at the gates of the odd palace and left me there. Its peaceful exit was not my first clue that this entire event was planned, it wasn't even the most significant clue, but it was a clue all the same. I had seen the things circle Ari as I bounced upside down against the Trolls ass and knew this was a targeted strike.

Fucking Trolls.

Fucking Queen.

I sat in front of a mirror dressed in a long silver gown that dipped to show my cleavage. It fit my curves perfectly, and a long slit showed my muscular legs. A small train trailed behind the platinum accented and decorative glass-covered thing. It weighed a ton. My mess of odd hair was piled on my head, and my dark skin shined in the pale light from the sconces on the wall. Gold flecked eyes stared back at me and wondered again about this strange turn.

I'd been here three months, time enough to acclimate to their language and pass several tests given to all warrior females. Never had I imagined this place existed. Never had I heard of the Eruhini or Eregion, yet these people are our cousins from the old days. The Winter Court to the Fae Summer, so says their Queen.

It is a strange land of ice and snow. The winter is harsh and endless. Tall spires of ice and mountains block the sky and surround a palace made of burnished black stone. A town surrounds the palace that, from the windows high above, appears almost normal. Almost.

These people are all the same. I stand out in the sea of either silver, white, or black hair and pale skin like a beacon. I've fought my way through their ranks with each test they give and have found that they are true warriors.

Were Ari here, she would have killed the Queen and been home with her men already, but my skills with a sword are not as sharp, so I only made it to Second Sword, whereas the

Queen is First. Many a warrior was stunned by me. All of them can kiss my ass.

If they were thinking to steal a weak Fae female, they screwed up. Big time. Though Ari is better with a sword, I am better with my fists and heavier weapons like maces and the ax.

Females here are not as rare as they are in Talamh na Sithe, but they are still significantly outnumbered by the males. However, in this cold land, women rule everything. It's odd. Not the only odd thing, but a very odd thing.

According to Queen Kharis, they need to add some diversity to their population and hoped that stealing a few Fae females would do it. They wanted Airmed and two other girls. That they know of Ari at all was the biggest clue as to how this transpired.

Queen Kharis looks like a silver-haired version of The Queen of Talamh na Sithe, Aramea. She has a black streak running through her wavy silver hair, and her eyes are blue, not green, but the similarities are there. She shares the same cold looks and dark glares, and I know they are related, perhaps even sisters.

Not even when I bested her warriors in testing has she been unkind or threatening. Still, the propensity for violence is there in her eyes. Those eyes met mine in the mirror as I placed the last touch of paint on my lashes.

"You look stunning. Every male in the pen will clamor to serve you," she said, walking to me and placing her fair hands on the silver fabric of my dress. The contrast against my skin is stunning. At home, I would wear red or other bright colors, but I have to admit the silver is not bad; it's just not something I would have chosen.

"Thank you, my Queen," I said, reverting to my formal tone with her. My stomach dropped at the thought of what was to come; I didn't agree with any of it.

"I've told you hundreds of times to call me Kharis, none of that formal my Queen stuff, please. This is not Talamh na Sithe, and I am not my sister," she said, confirming my suspicions.

"Kharis, thank you for the dress; it's lovely." I moved to stand, but she placed her hands on my shoulders and used her strength and size to keep me in my seat.

I'm not tall, not like Kharis, but I am not short like Ari, either. I mean, no one can be short like Ari, but I'm not tall like most Fae or Erhu either.

"I'm glad to see it covers your tattoos," she added, bringing a rueful smile to my face.

I was dropped at the gates in the Spring while there was still snow and ice on the ground. Once summer had reached its height and the snow melted, I ventured outside to put my bare feet into the warm, sparse grass and was taken to the ground by the flow of magic.

My keepers had watched in horror as magic tattooed my skin from the toes on my left foot up and over my hips and back around to my arm. Only the left side was marked. Out of all the strange things, this may have been the most bizarre.

The tattoo is silvery-white on my darker skin and made of beautiful swirls in continuous lines from toes to fingers. The design is ancient-looking and triggered something deep in my hindbrain to turn on and function. I have no idea what they are for, but they are there all the same. The Queen had not been happy about any of it.

In Eregion, only slaves have tattoos, yet I am not a slave.

The slit in my dress exposed my right leg, not the left. Although most know the tattoos are there, Kharis wants them covered.

Her hands rested heavily on my shoulders a moment before she lifted them. "Your trials are through, and tonight we accept you as one of our own. You've earned your place as my second blade, my first fighter, and my third anvil. Had I known what a warrior you are, I would have shown the Trolls your drawing and commanded they retrieve you specifically. They chose well. We are honored." I watched her vacant eyes, not sure I believed her.

I missed my friends, that's true enough, but that's all I missed. I'd been in two households in a short time and had nothing to show for it. I had been given to a total of eight men and was still a virgin. None had been unkind, and for that, I am grateful.

In the first home, the men had been together so long that they could not accept a female into their lives. They had dressed me up like a doll, done my hair, and treated me kindly, but they had no interest at all in a sexual relationship. They wanted a daughter, not a wife.

The Queen came one day and demanded that she view a mating, saying it was an old custom, and she needed to confirm that our contract could be fruitful. The men had lain down, cradled me, held my hands, held one another's hands, cried, cajoled, and pleaded, but they could not perform the act. They all sobbed and clung to each other as I was taken from them.

In the second place, the men planned to take a few days for us to become accustomed to one another. The Trolls saw to it that there would never be a chance to consummate our relationship.

Here? Goddess, are things different.

"Ready, Teagan Rilynoquar?" the Queen said, standing straight and tall while drawing me from my thoughts.

She had changed my surname to make up for the fact that my name was very Fae sounding and not at all Erhuhini. Once my trials were completed, the other warriors had chosen for me. They say it means House of The Fist, for that is what I am to them now. A fighter. First Fist. Funny how my sister is the same in Talamh na Sithe, only no one knows it but The Eight.

"Yes, Kharis. I'm ready." There was no choice, I thought as I rose from the chair and strode behind her from the room.

The Palace is immense. It took me the better part of my time simply to find the Throne room. I'd been granted a large suite of rooms in an empty, unused section of the place. Everything I could want and more than I need is available to me. There is more wealth here than I imagined possible.

We walked down marble halls with platinum, crystal, and mirrored accents. The sword strapped to my back rustled softly as I went.

This land has electricity. It took me weeks to figure out I did not need candles or flames to light my way or heat my food; I had only to flip a switch or turn a knob. They use torches and candles for effect, but there is no need.

The water for my baths is always hot, and they have fountains from the walls of their bathing rooms that emit a stream of water they call a shower. It's insanity. They trade goods with other realms and brought this so-called technology back with them. I can't say it's a bad thing.

When I'm settled, as they say, I will take a house of my own. Until then, I stay in the palace occupying more space than one person or six could use alone.

Like everything else, that would change.

I followed the swish of the Queen's skirts and the lights glinting off the sword across her back down the stairs and into the Great Hall. Talamh na Sithe has one of these too, but it smells like pain and old blood. This hall is twice the size of that one and smells like fresh pine and newly fallen snow.

Every warrior in the land lines the walls. Hundreds of women in silver and white stand at attention, swords strapped to their backs and tall glaives in their hands. The blades on the glaives gleam and reflect the light so that the contents of the makeshift pens in the center of the room are highlighted by ever shifting bright spots.

Men crouched at the sides of their Warriors and in the pens crowding the center of the room, moved here tonight for just this purpose.

"Tonight, we welcome Teagan Rilynoquar, First Fist, Second Blade, and Third Anvil; long may she live!" Kharis announced, her voice booming out across the vast space.

"Long may she live!" the warriors said in unison, their voices loud enough to shake the delicate glass pieces hanging from the chandeliers above the floor.

"Warriors all, add your blood to the cup, and we'll drink for our health!" Taking her sword and holding it high, the Queen sliced across her palm and let a few drops of blood dribble into a large silver cup set on a dais at the front of the hall.

Each woman came, repeating the process until the cup was full. As they passed me, they stopped, gripping my forearm with theirs and leaving bloody prints on the bared skin of my right arm.

When at last it was my turn, I took my sword and added my blood to theirs.

"Daughters of Eregion," Kharis started, stopping to allow for the single thump each woman made with her glaive upon the marble floor. "We unite to accept and welcome Teagan into the ranks of the best warriors in all the lands. May she fight hard, bear many daughters, and die covered in the blood of her enemies." The Queen shouted the last bit, and the room erupted into raucous cheers. Woman pounded their glaives onto the floor until the din was breathtaking.

Inwardly, I rolled my eyes. There hadn't been a battle since I'd been here. The women trained and worked, but the place had been nothing but peaceful since my arrival.

Picking up the cup, the Queen brought it to my lips, tilting it so that my only recourse was to drink or wear a bloody gown. I took one gulp of the viscous stuff, choking it down. I was grateful when she pulled the cup away and brought it to her lips. When she finished, the women rushed forward, grabbing for the cup so that each might sip our joined blood.

Fights broke out, and cheers rose, filling the hall with so much noise that the bones in my ears vibrated. I stood side by side with the Queen and watched the cup get passed around until it was empty, and the women were once again lining the walls.

"And now you must choose your House. Three men to serve you through the days of their life. They are yours until their death. As they provide for your needs, you provide for their safety. Their decisions are yours to make. Their punishments yours to bear. Choose wisely." Kharis opened the gate to the pen, where men knelt, separated into groups of three. "It's smarter to pick bonded Trios, but if a particular slave strikes your fancy, I will remake a Trio to include it.

And here was the part of all this I dreaded. For months I had known it would come to this. I didn't care about the ceremony, the blood, or even being here. I liked this place. I fit in, despite my coloration.

I enjoyed the freedom that came with being female in this place. I had no desire to run home through Troll country to regain what? Friendships I was practically forbidden to enjoy? No, I liked it here just fine.

I walked through the groups of men, their pale skin oiled and shimmering in the lights above. They wore paneled leather skirts that separated into sections as they knelt, and thin studded straps crisscrossed their chests and backs. Their muscles danced and twitched from the effort it took to kneel for this length of time. Their hair was a mix of silver, black, or both, just like everyone else. There was minimal color among their ranks, except for a few other women they had stolen from one place or another. And me; I imagined they'd never seen anything like me before.

I didn't want to own men, I could barely take care of myself, yet they expected me to pick out a Trio of slaves to provide for. I didn't think it was right, but I kept my thoughts on the matter to myself. It was the only thing about Eregion I found distasteful. Had I wanted a choice in Talamh na Sithe? Of course, I had. The opportunity to walk my path was one thing; this type of choice was something else entirely.

Keeping my face blank and my eyes forward, I walked through them. "Eyes up where I can see them," I commanded. In this place, appearances are everything. I had to appear strong. I had to appear commanding. In other words, I had to fake it 'till I made it.

Some of the men reached out to touch the hem of my gown, others shook where they knelt, and others watched me as directed. Here and there, I allowed my hand to trail over a shoulder or brush aside long hair. I used my left hand and not my right. After being tattooed, sometimes, I felt things.

What does one do with three male slaves? In this land, whatever one wants.

Their tattoos were not like mine. Where mine are delicate and twisting things, theirs were darker, primal, and masculine.

Rods pierced their nipples, and all were waxed free of hair unless the men here did not grow it. They were bare as babes, not that I'd ever seen one of those either, I just assumed.

I ruffled straight hair and skimmed bald heads, feeling nothing. My newfound ability gave me no insight as to which Trio to choose. I didn't want any Trio. At least not like this, but it was the price to pay for being in Eregion and was not optional. I was on the backside of the middle row when I met the bright gray eyes of a man with long silver hair braided down his back and felt something travel down my spine and settle in my core.

I had asked all the men to keep their eyes raised. Few had been able to do it, and those who did kept them fixed on some spot ahead. This man met my eyes as I looked across the others' backs, and I found that intriguing. The two other men in the Trio had their eyes up as well, taking me in, but stopping short of looking at my face.

One of them had blue eyes, which are rare here. Blue eyes are royal eyes, most people had gray or silver eyes, but his eyes were strikingly blue. Black hair skimmed his shoulders, and a stripe of pure white ran through the hair at his temple.

The other man had eyes that looked black from this distance. The black hair that lay pulled into a loose knot at the base of his neck had a gentle wave to it. They were, by far, the most interesting group to me.

Walking over to them, I trailed my hands down the spine of the silver-haired man who still pinned my eyes, feeling electricity shoot through my hand, down the tattoos, and through my toes. I kept my surprise to myself.

A muffled grunt from him had the Queen swinging a leather tipped whip against his side. "Eyes down and be silent," she said, letting her whip hit him twice, sending my blood boiling.

"This Trio will do nicely," I said, modulating my voice so that my fury didn't show.

"I suggested you choose wisely, Teagan; these are not the wisest choice. Their former owner bore many a scar on her back as she was unable to keep them in line." She raised her whip again and moved to strike the man a third time.

"I like a challenge, My Queen, they are mine now. Stay your hand, if you will. He is mine to punish," I reached for the man's chin, turning it left and then right as if to inspect it. "If there are to be marks on him, I will place them," I finished. His eyes narrowed on mine, and I gave him a little wink, making sure no one but he could see it.

The Queen chuckled low, as did several women lining the walls. "Ah, Teagan, you will need this more than I." She passed me her whip, and I took it, knowing I couldn't do anything else.

"Thank you," I said, moving in beside the men. I walked forward, they followed. I did not look down to check, it was expected, and they would do it.

Kharis taught me that all men are slaves from birth. I didn't like it, but it wasn't my culture, and it wasn't my place to change it. As long as these men did not get me whipped for their mistakes, I would treat them like the people they were.

"And now we eat and dance!" Kharis raised her arms and swept them wide.

Strange music played, accented by the sound of many drums and the echoes of something ancient and primal. Tables laden with rich and fragrant food wheeled into the room, their domed lids removed to reveal dishes the likes I had never seen.

The men rose, retreating to the walls while the women came forward, taking drinks off of trays being passed around the room by men dressed in little more than short skirts, the piercings in their oiled bodies glinting in the room's light. I stood unsure, not moving forward and not moving back.

"Go eat, or they'll notice," I looked down and found that the Trio of men still knelt at my feet, one of them having spoken the words quietly so as not to attract attention. Which one I could not tell.

"Well, then go stand with the others, I guess. I won't be long," I answered, looking at their bent heads and trying to decide who had spoken.

"We cannot. Not until after this night can we stand." My eyes found the black-eyed man's, and I nodded in understanding.

"This place is odd; I don't know that I'll ever understand the finer points of it. Very well," I sighed. "I'll go. Stay away from the others if you will. I don't want to see whip marks when I come back." I gave them a stern look. I didn't want to own men, but I had learned how things ran here well enough to know I had to say something to them.

The blue-eyed one chuckled, drawing stern looks from a warrior near enough to hear. I stalked away, heading to the heavy tables and drink servers.

Chapter Two

Syl'ta

We watched her weave through the crowd of starkly beautiful women. Only beauty can trick you. Just because a thing is pleasing to the eye does not mean it is welcoming to the heart. I know these women. There is no kindness here, no beauty beyond the depth of skin. The strange woman with skin like hot tea and cinnamon walked through them, and the fiercest Erhu warriors made way for her.

She was electric. Heat surrounded her as if she were a hearth filled with hardwoods and soft pine. She was foreign, one of the Queen's stolen ones, yet she did not quake and tremble the way most of them did. I have never seen anything like her.

Our last mistress died in a battle far away, or so Kharis said. We went to the pens where I had hoped to remain for the rest of this wretched life, but now, I was rethinking that hope. This new mistress was unlike anything around her, and I wondered if I was the only one who could see it. A glance at my brothers showed me they saw it too.

A dragon among wolves is what she is, and they don't appreciate the danger that ripples tantalizingly from her. From my vantage point, I can see the tattoos on her leg, and I wonder what manner of creature she is and from where she was stolen. My sister would have been better served to leave her.

She reached for the drink a kitchen slave offered, sparing him no glance though he looked at her longer than he should. Her gaze swept over the women and lit on her Trio, catching us watching. She moved on as if she found us uninteresting before glimpsing the giant throne of ice that resided at the front of the room. She stared at it, and I stared at her.

"Eyes down Slave," A sharp crack to my ribs had me lowering my eyes, but not before I caught the flush of anger that crossed our new mistress's young face. She moved our way, but before she could reach us, the offending warrior moved on, losing herself in the crowd.

We are like children. A village raises us, and a village can break us. I stilled, keeping my eyes on the floor in front of me. I would not put this new one in a situation she does not fully comprehend. They may have taught her the customs of this place, but they did not teach her the intricacies, I have no doubt. The slaves aren't the only things these warriors try to break.

Though they need the new blood the stolen ones bring, they do not enjoy being bested by them, and rumors run like wild things through the slave pens. The new stolen one is fierce. But she is something else too, something other. Magic drips from her like heart blood. Funny that these warriors can't sense it.

17

Superiority has a price, and it is one they don't know they are paying.

She circled back, casting sidelong glares at the warrior who hit me on the side. I caught her eyes and saw her fire. In a battle between fire and ice, there can be no winner. Fire melts the ice, but given time, ice turns to water and extinguishes the fire. This odd warrior was full of flames and encased in a frozen land. It flared in her amber eyes, the black ring around them growing thicker or thinner with emotion. It flamed in her wild hair as she moved and breathed. She was a firestorm brought to life.

She is regal.

Seasoned warriors moved from her path instinctively, then grew furious at the force she exuded over them.

They were fools. Whatever conveyance used to get this wild thing here should be used post haste to take her back. She would break this world, and only the voiceless among us could see it.

I caught the eyes of the Trio of men next to us and saw the same realization on their faces. Looks flew like snow on a breeze around the room, from slave to slave, Trio to Trio. We communicated a warning about this new warrior.

Where she went, blood would follow.

Chapter Three

Teagan

"Anxious to play with your new toys?" A warrior named Ang'ali slipped from the crowd, stopping by my side.

"They are stunning. Why shouldn't I be?" I said, not sparing the Trio a glance and keeping my eyes on the woman beside me. I had won the place as Second Sword from her, and she had not been pleased by the loss.

"Fuck them often, as it keeps them docile. The blue-eyed one is trouble as he is unbroken, although many warriors have tried. The silver-haired one has a strong will and a wicked tongue," she stopped with a chuckle. "In many ways, his tongue is wicked. The dark one is bland and boring. At least you'll have one male you won't take the lash for," she finished, bringing me into an awkward side hug that made me want to kill her. They were men, not horses. It was disgusting to speak of them this way.

"Thank you for the advice, Ang," I replied, knowing she hated it when I shortened her name.

I walked away, giving her my back and feeling her hard stare on it. I piled a plate high with some roasted meat at the table and used my fingers to shove it into my mouth.

For all their strength and technology, they are but savages. I watched as the Queen made rounds through the throngs of her warriors. Their eyes glittered, and fingers tensed. These people had built a culture around war and, now that there was no war, they chafed. This place was a match ready to light. It wouldn't take much to set it on fire.

I finished my meat and piled another plate full, pretending to pick at it. Then I added some delicate-looking pastries to the side and hoped they were like Ari's. No, I prayed, they were like Ari's. "You there," I said, calling to the Trio and pointing at the blue-eyed one. "Stand and take this; I don't wish to carry it."

A chuckle sounded behind me, "Leaving already?" I turned to find Kharis watching me with narrowed eyes.

"Yes," I said, adding nothing more.

"Which one are you taking first?" she asked, surprising me. "You're not a virgin, are you? If so, you need to see one of the warriors before you allow them to serve you."

The lie flowed smoothly on my tongue, "Of course not," I said, tilting my head, feigning thought, "I think I'll have him first." Something strange happened when I left Talamh na

Sithe; I learned that I could lie. In my homeland, only a few can outright lie. Aramea and Ari lie seamlessly. Now, so can I.

I trailed my hands across the muscled planes of the blue-eyed man's stomach, feeling the electric spark between us again.

"Interesting choice. The dark one would be better, though. That one serves well and rarely speaks, making it a more enjoyable experience. Remember not to confuse them with other Erhus; you don't want them to get ideas about their station. They are here to serve our needs and no more," she said, her gaze sliding over the men in front of me, pausing on the man I had claimed as my first.

"Yes, of course," I said, bowing my head at the Queen in apology. "Take it." I thrust my plate at him and walked away, not sparing them a glance because I knew they were behind me.

Chapter Four

Kar

Great Gods above, what has happened to us now? I watched as Syl rose to take this new terror's plate and pad behind her like a gentle lamb. Lyrolas and I stood to follow, shooting worried glances at one another.

They used to make us crawl on our knees, but that caused too much damage to the joints, keeping us from being optimal performers and shortening our work span. Syl doesn't so much as cut his eyes at her, and I worry what has happened to him.

She is beautiful, but he is not one to be swayed by looks. There is something about her I have not encountered before. She radiates warmth, where the others have none. Her face glowed, and her dark cheeks burned at the apple where the pink shined through. Her crazy hair moved around her face on its own accord, and I sensed that she is wild, feral, and alien.

I wonder where they stole her.

She moves with deadly grace, and thick muscles in her legs show their definition through the slit in her dress, and her strange tattoos peek out as she strode with purpose away from us.

We rounded the corner away from the eyes of others, and she stopped. Her shoulders slumped, her head tilted back, and she took a deep breath before continuing at a slower pace. Syl keeps perfect pace behind her. Lyrolas says nothing; he just takes it all in.

A day Lyros is speechless is not a good day. It might be a safe day, but it is not a good day.

Sighing, I followed the silent figure down mirrored halls and through silvered doors. For one so new to this massive maze of a place, she knows her way around. I caught the scent of her like some strange flower mixed with an undertone of iron or maybe the sharp tang of New World steel.

Perhaps she would change her mind and pick me first, as the Queen suggested. I wondered if she was as hot on the inside as the waves coming off of her suggested.

We were in the furthest reaches of the palace now, down unused halls and passed long-empty rooms. I wonder if our Mistress knew that she'd been placed in an area long forgotten and if she cared about what that might imply. A little-known fact about slaves is that just because we aren't permitted to speak doesn't mean we can't hear. We had all heard of our Mistress's prowess with her fists and a sword.

Other males in the pens begged to be chosen by her, thinking that perhaps her strength equated to their safety. They forget that the Queen goes through the pens like mad and discards more slaves than the land can replace, and she is the strongest of them all. Strength does not equal safety. Not for males. Not in this land.

I wondered if we would survive the night.

Technically, it is a crime to kill one's slaves. Still, that technicality matters not when the punishment is so minor that the crime happens regularly.

At the end of the hall was a great door, and she pushed through it without thought and care. I knew these quarters. They belonged to a long-dead King, and I wondered anew as to what the presence of this molten warrior might mean.

Things weren't always this way.

She sighed, kicking her spiked shoes off and letting them fly into the wall beyond. Her quarters were a mess, clothes piled on the floor, and mismatched shoes lay along the base of every wall as if it were her habit to come in and kick them off in such a manner.

The entry led to an ornate, well-furnished sitting area. Every surface was draped with discarded clothes like she enters the place and can no longer stand to be dressed.

Closed doors shielded other rooms from view, and I knew from old books that the ancient king had multiple sleeping areas for his concubines. These areas were explored by many an unguarded slave, and rumors of the opulence of them passed from mouth to ear over time, as the dream of ever being free men again died.

French doors into the main sleeping area were open, and the giant-sized bed was piled high with blankets, furs, and other cast-off from this strange woman.

"Thank the Goddess that's over." She moved behind us, shutting the door and barring it.

We three stared at each other with unconcealed shock.

"You can eat that. Sorry I didn't get more, but I was trying to be inconspicuous. There is some dried meat, nuts, bread, and water on the sideboard; help yourselves. I'm going to get out of this Goddess damned dress and wash this day off because it sucked." She stopped, laughing and tossing her head so that her wild curls bounced with a life of their own.

"I can run you a bath, milady," Lyros said, finding his voice but using it oddly. I turned to him so sharply my neck hurt. Lyros is not known for his gentle words, and it stunned me to hear him speak them. He rarely offers anything and makes whatever warrior who owns us work for his compliance.

"Thank you, but that will be unnecessary. Make yourselves comfortable." She flipped a hand in the general direction of the room and walked away.

We knelt with our heads bowed when she shut the door to the bathing room.

"What kind of creature is she?" Lyros asked, hissing through clenched teeth.

"How am I supposed to know?" I answered, my voice shaking from fear. If she heard our soft words, she could punish us.

"I'm telling you; she is something new; I feel the power coming from her. She is not like the other stolen ones. She might survive," Syl said, his voice a steel knife penetrating my heart with hope.

I was tired of weakness.

I was also tired of hope as it hurts far more than despair.

"Don't get your hopes up, Syl. She could be like all the others," I cautioned, keeping my eyes on the closed door between our Mistress and us. We could hear her swearing incessantly at the 'motherfucking dress.' "Should we do something? She seems unable to get undressed."

"No. It could be a test. We wait," Lyros said, watching the door as if it might explode outward at him.

We heard the sounds of fabric tearing and crystals and glass hitting the floor. A chuckle followed, then the sound of water falling. On our knees, we waited to see what manner of creature owned us now.

Chapter Five

Teagan

Wrapped in a soft dressing gown, I came out of the bathing room to find the Trio on their knees with heads bent. "I told you to be comfortable; that does not look comfortable. For Goddess's sake, get up, eat, relax, whatever. None of this on your knees business, not here."

I watched as they rose, keeping their eyes down.

"What are your names?" I asked. The darker one's breath hitched, and he took a pained gasp. His black eyes flew to mine, momentarily holding my gaze. They are given names at birth, I know this, even if it's only, so their wardens have some way to yell at them.

They looked at one another, and I rolled my eyes. "It's a simple question," I said. "You may speak freely."

"Mistress..." the silver-haired one started, but I refused to start out hearing an explanation from them.

"My name is Teagan; you will call me by my name. Whatever you need to do out there," I paused, waving a hand in irritated defiance at the door, "Do it. Here, I am Teagan. I think it's repugnant to own slaves, so I will not own you. Here, you are men. Your names, please?" Their heads whipped around so quickly I worried they might fly off. If entire conversations could be shared with just looks, they shared them. I waited as they stared at one another but said nothing.

I had all night.

I went to the dresser in the corner of the largest bedroom, eyeing them through the open French doors as they stayed locked in silent conversation. I dropped my robe and felt their eyes turn to me. I didn't care about nudity, not even a little bit. I know how I look. I've always been muscular.

I've often complained to my sisters that so many muscles shouldn't be on so small a body, but nothing can be done for it. The months I spent here have only increased the size and definition of them. My tattoos accentuate their curves and edges, swirling and highlighting the strength in my body. If anyone had ever noticed, they might think it sexy. The Trio behind me noticed.

I moved around the room naked, picking through clothes and vowing silently to straighten up. Pulling a short chemise over my head, I straightened my mass of errant curls in the mirror before they would force me to turn back to them and order them to tell me their names.

Movement in the mirror caused me to freeze. I leaned forward, no longer seeing myself but a verdant path ahead. I heard my name and glanced over my shoulder, knowing the sweet voice in my ear did not come from one of the Trio. They watched me but seemed to hear nothing. I heard my name again. Raising my hand to the mirror, I touched the cool surface and was pulled through.

I watched in horror as the men rushed to the mirror and began pounding on it. I beat back, but they didn't see me. I hit the glass with all my might, and it didn't so much as shimmer. Turning, I placed my back to the mirror so as not to leave it unguarded. I had no weapons other than my fists and was barely dressed. Barefoot and wary, I slid down the path on silent feet.

The air was warm and sweet-smelling, and I took a minute to breathe it. Though the snow may melt for a few cycles of the moon, it never gets truly warm in Eregion. There is always a hint of a chill. This place is the winter court in more than just name.

I filled my lungs with warm air, and the smell of flowers hit me hard. It smelled like home; the sweetest places in Talamh na Sithe would smell like this for months at a time.

I'm lost yet found.

"Fear not, Teagan; you are safe here." The voice was louder now that I was through the glass.

"I'll be the judge of that," I answered, toeing my way closer and closer to the location of the voice.

I walked around a curve in the path where the foliage was so thick it obscured my view. Huge, bright yellow flowers as large as my head dipped from vines hanging in trees as tall as the sky. I was stunned to silence by the beauty.

The pull was strong. I wanted to stop and stare at the tiny bird with four wings beating so fast that they looked like they weren't moving, but I couldn't. I could only put one foot in front of the other or fall and be dragged.

Purple blooms, orange blooms, green blooms, and red assaulted me with their brightness and bold smells. I stopped breathing. I had an idea where I was and who beckoned me closer, but I had no idea as to why.

The final step on the dense path took me into a meadow so green it did not look real. Horses of every color grazed by a clear, blue lake, and birds, like I had never seen, flew overhead.

"Teagan, I'm glad you came." The Great Goddess and Maker of All Things stood just to the left of the path I stumbled off. She was resplendent with lavender eyes and long silver hair. She was naked, and the sun shined off the pale skin of her body.

Her hair blew in lazy strands around her face, and she glowed with ethereal beauty.

She was smaller than I expected.

Not that I ever expected to meet her.

The Goddess used to walk among her people, even mating with the men and having children, or so the old tales say. She has not walked with us for a while. Some say Aramea killed the one she loved most, causing her to forsake the rest. No one knows for sure.

As little girls, The Eight would stare in wonder at the walls of the Great Hall and note that the place smelled like sour magic and old blood. It was tainted beyond repair by foul deeds and suffering. It is whispered that the pain came from the Goddess's truly born son, and for that, we suffer.

We used to play a game where we would guess what happened, and each girl would build upon it the most fantastical tales. Often shocked by the twisted stories we told one another on stormy nights by the light of a lone candle, we likely never got close to the truth.

Cedar and pine cannot rid that hall of the scent of dark magic permeating the air. I drop to my knees and lower my eyes.

"For my sake, get up," she laughed with the sound of a thousand bells. "I mean it; up you go."

I rose without trying.

"Goddess…"

"Call me Dani; I insist."

"I."

"Yes, you can."

"Um."

"Yes," she said with finality, and I supposed yes, it was. She is the Goddess; you can't fight that.

"Okay," I said, still not meeting her eyes.

"Let's walk," she said. She turned, and I followed.

"This place is beautiful," I said, scanning the meadow and the lake again, admiring its beauty. Insects chirped, and horses blew air through their noses, making soothing sounds that traveled across the field despite the stillness of the air.

"Thank you, it's one of my favorites," she said, looking out at the beauty surrounding us. Her silver hair flowed around her body, moved by a breeze I couldn't feel.

"You're wondering why you're here," she started as we approached the still water that was so clear you could see fish swimming below the surface.

"I suppose I am." I crept to the side of the lake and ran my toe through the water, chasing away a fish, my calm words hiding the fact that my heartbeat was like the wings of that strange bird. She laughed out loud, her head tilting back, so the sun caught her long silver lashes, making them glitter.

"Ever the cool one." She smiled, her entire face open and warm. "Your path has not been an easy one, nor has it been kind, and for that, I apologize; it has, however, been necessary."

"My path has had many forks but has not been unkind," I said, tilting my face to the sun and allowing it to warm me. I hadn't felt anything like this since Trolls took me.

"I'm glad you feel that way, and there are more forks to come, I am afraid. Though I cannot entirely affect your future, I have set in place many things to guide you where I wish you to go. You still have choices, and they are yours. But inasmuch as I can, I have great plans for you." She turned the full power of her lavender gaze on me, and I had trouble standing in the power of it.

"I don't understand," I said, sliding to the grass and stretching out my legs so they could get sun too. My tattoos tingled when they connected with the ground while strength hummed through my muscles.

"And that's okay." My Goddess joined me on the ground.

Around us, animals shuffled, adjusting their positions to accommodate us. None of them were close, but their awareness of us was evident by the twitch of an ear here and the rise of a head there.

"Magic boils from Eregion ground, yet they have forgotten me. Sisters divided my people, each liking their ways more than mine. They think their power is omniscient and their rule unending. They are wrong. Sisters will bring my lands together again and rejoin my people as One, and then we will be strong."

"Here, where there is more magic than the land can recycle, these people have forgotten that we are One People. They have forgotten they have magic, trusting only the strength and might of their blades. Where I had forsaken the People of Talamh na Sithe, here, they have forsaken me. Yet in Talamh na Sithe, I ripped their futures from them to assuage my anger and grief, but they worship me still."

"I destroyed their land, their magic, and their lives; still, my name is upon their lips. I am ashamed of myself. One group took my son from me, and I made the entirety of my People pay for it."

"Any mother would have done the same," I said before I could stop myself. "Any mother with power would have razed the world and made it anew so that her son could live again. They got off easy," I said, trying to let the compassion I felt for her loss bleed into my voice so that it might soften the steel. It's mentioned on more than one occasion that I am far too direct. It's a constant effort to temper that.

"Your heart is strong, young one," she laughed, her smile reaching her eyes and making small lines around them.

I have never seen anything more beautiful than my Goddess smiling.

"But no. I was wrong. I accept responsibility for my actions and have begun the slow process of fixing them, and that is where you come in. Winter Court or Summer Court, Light or Dark, they are *my* courts. They were designed to be ruled separately but remain together. They were to pay homage to me, not to individual rulers. The Sisters are not omniscient, even I am not. I am their Goddess; they are not your Goddesses."

"Sisters will fix what I have broken. The land will heal. Our People will be One again under better stewards than Kharis and Aramea. You will see to that. You and Airmed will see to that," she finished, the fierceness of her statement echoed off the ground around us, and I could feel the promise in it.

"Why me?" I whispered so low I was afraid she couldn't hear.

"Why not you?" She raised her head and caught my eye, and I saw steel in her gaze. "You are brave, strong, smart, and you see what is wrong with the world. Magic courses through you, and you know my name. You are the one. My faith and every confidence rest on you girls. You will fix what is broken."

"I wouldn't know where to start," I said, shaking my head in denial. "I don't want to rule. I never dreamed of such a thing, not like Ari does."

"And that is why you will be a great ruler, Teagan. You've had nothing, no anchor except neglected and abandoned sisters. You've taught each other what no mother could. Compassion. Kindness. Piety. Love. Strength. Resolve. Had you been raised by the mothers of Talamh na Sithe, you would not have learned those things. You girls are the future but not in the way Aramea hopes. Not yet. I respect that about you. You will honor your people in ways she never could."

"I am honored, Great Goddess."

"Call me Dani." She plucked a flower out from the grass and brought it to her nose. After inhaling, she tossed the flower up, and it became a bright orange butterfly and fluttered away.

"Things are not always as they seem," she started. "You must remember that. I gave you immense power, more than even Airmed, for she will have help where you have none. Your tattoos guide the way. They provide anything you will need. From the soil, your power flows; let it flow through you. Do not fight it. Guide it, for it is yours to guide. Show the others the way or cut them down where they stand. My People must be One, or they cannot heal. Remind them what they have forgotten. Teach them they are Goddess blessed and that magic is theirs if only they remember. Make them remember my name. They will not thank you. Not at first. Watch your back. This road has the potential to be bloody and long."

"Your Trio of men will follow you if you treat them like what they are. Do not discount the help they offer but do not discount the treachery that lives in the hearts of those who do not want to see change take place. Even though their land is broken and twisted in ways Talamh na Sithe never has been, magic still bubbles from the ground. Take it. You'll need it."

"Someday, you will meet your Sister and her Daughter on the battlefield and destroy your enemies, for her Child's power could, perhaps, rival mine someday. There will be peace. I promise you. But first, there will be war. They cannot win without you. Know that. You are the lynchpin in plans that go far beyond Eregion, Teagan. Being Goddess blessed is a blessing and a curse."

"Dani, this seems impossible. All of it," I huffed, blowing a strand of my wild hair out of the way.

"Nothing is impossible, my daughter. You will prevail. The road may be long, and there will assuredly be pain, but you will prevail. I can't know everything, but I promise that much. She smiled again, and I saw just how magnificent a woman she is.

"I will do my best," I said, watching sprites dance and jump across the lake.

"You may come to the lake anytime. While here, time stops for you. You need a safe place, so I give you access to this one. No monsters reside here but do not travel beyond the edges of the meadow, for if you do, time will restart, and discovery of this plan will add danger.

"It's a lovely place, and I thank you," I said with a slight bow.

"You are welcome, my child. Return to Eregion and plot your course. I am here for you should you need me. Your Trio saw you fall through the portal, and although time has stopped, they are in the process of breaking my mirror." She gave a quiet chuckle, shaking her head. "You chose well." She reached up and kissed my cheek, and a sizzling warmth traveled down my face.

The tattoos came to life as lavender and silver sparks arced off them but caused no pain. I felt the power roll through their lines and continue until the silver light hit the ground below my bare feet and rippled out into the meadow beyond, marking this place as mine.

The animals in the area turned to look, striking curious poses. From where the Goddess once stood, a large, ornamental red bird rose from the ground and flew away with a single beat of her massive wings. She caught a current and circled lazily once before flying away.

I sat, even though she said I needed to return. I lay on the ground and let it calm me. Quiet power thrummed through the tattoos on my feet, cycling through their lines and returning to the ground as if on a circuit. I wondered if I would always need to be barefoot to have access to the magic coursing through me. In the land of ice and snow, that could prove to be problematic.

Sighing, I rose and wound my way from the edge of the lake to the path. The Goddess said that once I left the meadow, time would resume, so I hurried my steps in case the men were more successful at breaking the mirror than I had been.

I stepped through and grabbed the fists of the first man I could to stop him from hitting me instead of glass. I ducked to avoid the swing of a tool intended to break the mirror and rolled to a crouch in case they meant to turn their attack in my direction. They froze, dropping to their knees and clasping their hands behind their backs. Their heads hung, and not one eye turned my way.

Chapter Six

Lyros

The woman stepped through the mirror as if it was an everyday occurrence to step through mirrors. She must be a witch. I've heard of those strange women and the things they do to men.

There is a slave in the pens whose former owner captured him from another land because he caught her eye. He told me all about witches. This woman must be from those lands. She rose from a fighting stance and cut her strange eyes to me. I dropped mine, not wanting to be trapped by them.

She let them roam, looking for anything out of place, and while her attention was not on me, I took her measure. She is a small thing, yet so thick with muscle, she seems larger. I had never seen anything like her before. Her hair is a reddish-yellow wild mass of tight curls. Her eyes have planes to them, each a different color, so that you could not say whether her eyes were amber, gold, or otherwise. Her skin is a milky brown with a dash of red. She is nothing like the other women in this place. She contrasted even the ones they steal from far away realms. She was going to turn me into a frog; I just knew it.

I had hoped my smooth words and calm reaction earlier would help ease me peacefully into this new captivity. After seeing Teagan step from the mirror, I knew there was no saving any of us.

She rose, walking up to us. "Up, please. None of this kneeling business.

"Mistress," Kar said from his knees.

"None of that either. Up. Eat. Clean up. It's been a long day; don't make me give an order. Until we move elsewhere, this is our home. Here, we will act civilized."

"Are we not going to talk about the mirror?" Syl asked, making me want to punch him. He would end up a toad before me if he didn't shut his mouth.

"Not at this time," she answered, not looking at him. I watched as her brows clinched together. She smelled different now, like thunderstorms and sweet flowers grown in wild places.

She moved around the room, kicking at discarded clothing and muttering to herself. Syl rose to his feet, and Kar and I followed suit, casting worried glances at each other. Syl, ever the brave one, went and began to pick at the food she offered.

"My name is Lyrolas, Mistress," I said, bowing slightly in the direction of the tornado calling herself Teagan that ripped through the larger sleeping area.

"What a lovely name," she said, popping up from behind the bed and throwing a pile of dresses over her shoulder to smile at me. "Goddess, I hate dresses."

"Is there something specific you are looking for? Maybe we could help you find it." I said, and Syl almost tripped over himself at my newfound helpfulness.

She stopped with a sigh, "I am looking for a pair of riding pants." She dropped a pile of everything but riding pants onto the floor and stepped out of the ring she had made around herself. "We are riding to some Goddess forsaken section of this Goddess forsaken place. Kharis said I must go to ensure the 'peaceful cooperation' of whatever poor creatures live there," she finished, slumping onto the corner of the bed and throwing her eyes our way.

We had migrated to the food and were tearing through it like beasts. We hadn't eaten since breakfast.

"Must I ask for your names again, or are you going to tell me on your own?" she said, rising slowly and walking our way.

"My name is Syl'ta, and this is Thalakar. We call him Kar for short." Kar shot him a dark look and righted his face quickly when she glanced his way.

"Does Kar speak?" she asked.

"I speak," Kar said, bringing his eyes to hers but saying nothing else.

"Perfect. What duties are you expected to perform when not with me?" she asked, getting to the point.

"I work in the stables, Mistress," I offered first, unable to stop myself. I stifled a growl at my sudden compliance. A small note of it slipped past my lips, and I watched her notice.

"The horses hate him; it's quite funny," Syl said with a grin.

"What has made your lips so lose and your mouth so bold tonight, brother?" I asked, stalking towards him, the tension growing in my gut unbearable.

"Gentlemen," Teagan said. She stepped between us, placing her arms on our chests to stop our advance.

With one word, we stilled, lowering our eyes to the floor.

"It's been a long day for you as well, I'm sure. Eat your fill and shower if you like, but there will be no fighting." Dropping her hands, she moved away.

I glared at Syl and felt my lip curl up in a snarl. I needed a good fight, but the Lady was right; we could not do it here. He winked his twinkling eye at me, and I wanted to poke it out. What fresh torture was this? I wondered as I paced around the room, looking for riding pants to calm my nerves. Finding a pair that wasn't too wrinkled, I set them on the cleanest table in the room. Then I began to pick up the surrounding mess. How anyone could sleep in this pit was beyond me.

Syl covered his laugh with his hand and joined me in picking through the piles of clothes, and I knew for a fact he would be a newt before the end of the week. Our new mistress was most certainly a witch to have our tongues moving so freely, and she would soon tire of his brazenness.

"I work in the meat shops, cutting up what the hunters bring back," Syl said, cutting his sharp eyes at the woman rifling through a pile of shoes.

"Very good then. Are you handy with a knife?" she asked, dragging a pair of tall riding boots from beneath her discarded shoes.

"Not too handy, My Lady," he answered. Kar snorted water from his nose as he choked on his drink.

Syl was deadly with a blade. He'd proven that many times. Our first owner never returned from a hunting trip because of it. Her body was never found and never would be. We were aged only seventeen years back then, and he was already far deadlier than both of us put together.

Not that Kar and I hadn't had our moments.

We were known as an incorrigible Trio. The only reason we still lived was that Syl'ta was the Queen's younger brother, and she claimed to have a fondness for him. I had a feeling if we earned Teagan's displeasure, then the Queen's affection would reach its limit.

This was the end of the line for us.

"Kar works for the Smithy, Mistress," I offered with that dark thought in my head. "He helps make the finest weapons in all the lands.

"You mean he stokes the fires while the finest weapons in the land are made," Syl laughed, punching Kar in the arm, and Kar took a swing at him, but he ducked in time to avoid it.

Teagan chuckled, threw her boots near her riding pants, and sat on the bed. "I had brothers once that acted just like you," she said, and her face fell.

Quickly she rose and turned from us, digging through the clothes on the bed. I caught my brothers' eyes and shrugged. They shrugged back, and we continued to attempt to organize her mess. It would take us days to wash, fold, and right the place.

"Find what you need tonight, my Lady; we will organize your things tomorrow. You have all our time for a week before we return to our duties." I said, handing her a black shirt that would go with her riding pants and boots.

Grabbing it from my hands, she tossed it on top of the pants. Kar moved to smooth the fabric so she would not be such a mess in the morning as her appearance would now be a reflection of our usefulness.

"You must remember to call me Teagan," she said, turning back and catching us in the glare of her strange eyes.

"Mistress," Syl started. "Should we call you by your given name in front of anyone, it would mean punishment. I would prefer not to make that slip." He answered, clearing a corner of her room of debris and dragging a blanket onto the floor.

I watched as he arranged it so there were no wrinkles and then proceeded to find a few pillows from furniture and toss them onto the blanket. With a sideways glance at the woman, he lowered himself onto it, testing its softness.

"What are you doing?" she asked with narrowed eyes.

"Making our bed," he answered.

"I think not," she growled. "You will not be sleeping on the floor in the corner of my room when there are five or six empty beds."

Syl dropped a pillow and stole a glance at me. I couldn't help him understand because I didn't understand either.

With a sweep of her arms, the little devil cleared the clothing from her bed, grabbed a blanket from the pile, and eased onto the bed with a sigh. "Blow out the torches when you are done, please. I can't keep my eyes open any longer."

"Uh, my Lady, there are no torches. It is a switch," Syl started. "And, there is the matter of my beating that needs to be attended."

"I am not beating anyone," she said, rising from under the blankets with a scowl.

"You must," I said. "You stopped the Queen from punishing him earlier. You said that you would place the marks on his skin. She will check," I finished.

We all turned to face her expectantly.

Sighing, she got up. "I'm not beating you."

"I'll do it, brother," Kar said, picking up the whip the Queen gave our Mistress at the ceremony.

"No," Syl said, snatching the whip from his hand. "She must do it. She must learn, or we die. She must learn, or she dies, and I do not wish to start over. Not again."

"You know there is no starting over, Syl'ta. Not this time." I walked to him and took the whip from his hands.

He looked defeated for a moment, for finally, I said aloud what we all knew in our hearts. This was most certainly our last chance. It passed quickly, and he squared his shoulders.

Syl was responsible for our precarious position. Well, mostly anyway. His mouth and rash deeds paved the way for us as a Trio, but we loved him, and where he went, we followed.

Were we in any other land, Syl would be a prince and someday a king, but here, where men are possessions, he will die by his sister's hand for the traits his bloodline gave him.

"What land do you come from, My Lady," I said, stepping forward.

"I come from Talamh na Sithe," she said, her voice distant. I caught the faint tremor of her hand as she stood up by the bed, keeping it between us.

"The Court of Light." Kar's words came out in hushed surprise. "Bringing a Fae here is dangerous." He dropped his eyes and stepped back.

"Why would they do that?" I asked, turning to my brothers. We shared rapid fire thoughts between us as we often did in times of stress, forgoing words as they were too slow. And Teagan watched it all, saying nothing.

Syl moved with blinding speed and snatched the whip from Kar, stalking forward. The warrior did not cower from him. He was one and half times her size, and she stood her ground in the face of the violence that emanated out of him.

"Syl'ta," I yelled, trying to stop his forward progression. For as he stalked our new Master, death stalked him.

"No. She must understand this." He stopped, pushing the whip into her chest, forcing her to take it.

"You came from the Court of Light; never forget that. Never forget you are in the Court of Darkness. Those labels are more than literal; they are figurative as well. You will die if you do not understand that," he growled at her.

"You have no friends here," he continued, enunciating every word. "They will hate you for your beauty. They will hate you for your strength. They will hate you for the way you speak your thoughts. They will kill you for your conviction and burn you for your sense of right and wrong. And if you are Fae, truly Fae, they will kill you for your magic, for no magic lives here."

"Stop," I yelled, trying to pull him from her. He had crossed a line even a lenient warrior would not allow.

"They will kill you for the light inside of you they can never hope to have," he said, ignoring my pleas for restraint. "For the light fled this hell centuries ago. Trust no one, and if the Queen moves to beat me, never again stay her hand. Never. She will not kill me, and I can survive her better than you. Why they brought the Light Court here, I do not know, but their intentions are not good, Teagan Rilynoquar," he said, pushing her into the wall with his mass.

"Who are you?" she whispered, staring up at him with molten amber eyes.

"Who I am matters not." He leaned into her, crushing her mouth with his and causing her to give a startled cry. I strained to pull him off, already seeing my head on a pike by the palace gates.

He pulled away. Her chest rose and fell as she fought for breath. "Now, you must use that whip as the Queen will check my marks. If I don't feel the lash now, we will all suffer later." He walked to the center of the large main room and knelt with his back to her. He pulled the thin straps of leather down his shoulders so there would be no protection for his skin. "As the skin on my back is scarred, you must use your strength." He placed his knuckles on the marble floor to brace himself.

Kar and I knelt next to him as is our way. The lady's sharp intake of breath came out as a whimper, but despite her fear, she walked forward.

Chapter Seven

Teagan

The most beautiful man I'd ever seen gave me the kiss of a lifetime, my first kiss ever, and now he kneels at my feet, waiting for me to wield the whip in my hand against him.

I hate this place. I want to curl up in bed and cry. I want him to kiss me again. I want any and everything but to cover his deeply scarred back with more scars. The dim light of the room illuminates them, so they glow silver. There is nothing soft about them. They weave his back like a tale and crisscross the tops of his thighs in a gruesome kiss.

One tear falls from my eyes as I glide to him on silent feet, then another falls. I remember what the Goddess told me. She said that any magic I need is at my disposal, and I need this man to feel no pain as I mark his back. He did nothing to deserve punishment. He met my eyes, and that is all. There is no crime in that. Not anywhere normal anyway. This place is not normal.

The other men drop to their knees and stretch their backs in the same manner that Syl'ta did, and the whimper I tried to hold in escaped. He was right. I recognized my mistake with the Queen as soon as I made it, but it was too late. I could do this. If he could do it, I could do it. It only hurt my sensibility to punish him; it hurt his body.

At his side, I placed my hand on his strange hair, noting the purple highlights among the black strands. The white streak so clean that it shone. His hair felt like silk. I let my hand trail down his back; the scars felt like rope beneath it.

Taking a deep breath, I infused every bit of sunshine and warmth I felt by the lake in the mirror, every moment of peace I found there, I pushed into him. I felt his muscles relax, and a soft sigh escaped him.

I raised the whip, bringing it down sharply on his back. He did not flinch, but the two men next to him did. I reared back in horror. Is that what a bonded Trio meant? That they shared pain? I thought it meant they were friends, and they got along, but judging by the reaction to my first lash, it went deeper than that. Much deeper.

Focusing on my tattoos as the Goddess instructed, I pulled power from them, pushed it into Syl'ta, and brought the whip down again. None of them flinched this time. I worked quickly while the magic lasted. They shot confused glances at one another, and I pushed speed into my arm and marked him well. Tears fell down my cheeks, joining the blood my hand raised, and I cried.

I took for granted my safety. And my peace. I thought that since the Queen had not harmed me upon my arrival, this place might be home to me. I was wrong. The bold man in the land of enslaved men was right. How could he not be? He'd lived this life far longer than I.

With a shuddered breath, I stopped. The marks on his back were bloody and deep. Should the Queen check, she'd see proof of his punishment. My lashes were no kinder or gentler than the myriad others that came before them.

I dropped the bloodied whip at his side and backed away. Blood speckled my hands, and drops of it dried on my face.

"It will get easier, Teagan. I swear it will," Syl told me, keeping his face turned from mine.

"I hope it will not, Syl'ta, for if it does, I am lost." Locking myself in the bathroom, I stripped off the once white shift and threw it into the corner. Sobbing quietly, I washed the blood from my arms, watching the water run pink down the drain.

I couldn't stay here. Somehow, I had to get home. This place, their customs, I could not stay. I knew. I did. I'd seen enough in my short time here to understand that this was their way, but it wasn't mine. The Goddess said I would fix this land, but she was wrong. It is beyond redemption. I didn't want to fix it; I wanted to go home.

But then what.

Go back to a place where the Queen consorted with her sister to have Trolls take her daughter? Go back to my homeland, where women pass from house to house at the pleasure of a blood tainted Queen? Go home to bear a son that would be killed before his body could grow hair? That wasn't an option either. Sighing, I turned the water off, grabbed a towel, and went to face my waiting Trio.

The lights were off, and they lay curled at the foot of my bed. They were asleep, piled like kittens. The bed platform's immediate area was clean, and neatly folded clothes sat in stacks along the wall.

Shoes were paired, and towels hung. I stood for a moment and watched the slow, even rise and fall of their chests, wondering what sort of creature gets the skin stripped off their back then lies on the bed of the monster that held the whip. Leading me to ponder what sort of monster I was that I participated in their sick customs. I looked at the angry red flesh on Syl's back. The blood had dried, and they hadn't bothered to wipe it off. I did that.

Me.

The monster within is often scarier than the one roaming free.

Magic coursed through my tattoos, begging me to heal what I had harmed, but that wasn't an option. Slumping in my skin, I dropped my towel and crawled into bed. Pulling my knees tight to my chest, I burrowed under the covers and fell into a fitful sleep.

When I awoke, the men had showered and dressed, wearing the same leather studded skirts they had worn the day before. The straps crisscrossing their chests highlighted their pale skin and hard muscles. My eyes skimmed down their bodies to their legs and, finally, their bare feet.

They stood with their hands behind their backs and eyes down. Where was the fire I saw in them last night? I slid from the bed and watched as, one by one, their eyes found my body. They roamed freely. Goddess, they were beautiful, and I wanted them.

How I had been in three homes with eleven men and still not explored the pleasures muscular bodies can give was beyond me. But I wanted sex with men, not slaves. I wanted it badly; my body had been on fire for years with no relief but my own hand.

Sleep is the brain's time to reorganize and restructure. While I slept, resolve settled into every thought and corner of my mind. There was no going back to Talamh na Sithe. I needed to survive here. If the Goddess was right, and I had no cause to question a Goddess, then I needed to work to change this place.

A knock at the door pulled me from my thoughts. How long I stood there naked, I do not know, but the men still drank in my body with their eyes, and I smiled, moving toward them.

Shaking his head, Lyros handed me a long silken robe from under his feet. After everything they have been through, that a woman's body could still tempt them was beyond my understanding. But judging by the subtle rise of their leather skirts, they were tempted.

"My lady, the door," Lyros said, catching my eyes with his, and the gray of his iris almost obliterated by the black of his pupil,

"I don't care about the door," I whispered, dropping the robe and trailing my fingers down his chest. It was expected that I keep them docile; it was the Queen's order after all. I chuckled, tilting my face to his.

Another knock came, sharper than the first. Sighing, I snatched up the robe and moved to answer it. As I cracked the door open, the men dropped to their knees.

"Ah, Teagan, I thought I would come early and see how your first night with your new Trio went." Queen Kharis stepped through the door, pushing it wider. I said nothing as I belted my robe.

She walked behind my men, trailing her fingers along their shoulders. She stopped at Syl. Taking a nail, she dug it into one of the scabs my whip had caused. His body stiffened, and so did his brothers'. Fresh blood trickled from the wound, and I wanted to kill her where she stood.

"Nice work, Teagan; I doubted you could follow through with your word." Her finger dug deeper, popping open the scab, causing the wound to bleed freely.

I remembered what he said last night and measured my words carefully. "The scars were so thick that it was more challenging work than I imagined. Do be mindful of the pattern I laid out; it took planning and thought. I would hate to have it ruined.

"Very well," she sighed. "I can appreciate that. Did you fuck him?" she asked, coming to face Syl'ta. She took a long, pointed nail and dug it into the soft tissue under his chin, forcing his face up. She met his eyes and gave him a crooked grin. How a smile can be devoid of warmth, I don't know, but it was. I wondered, again, who he was. Seeing them side by side, royal eyes to royal eyes, I thought I knew.

"I did not, to be honest, the day was long. By the time it was over, I just wanted to sleep," I answered, immediately knowing it was the wrong thing to say. By the look on the Queen's face, I knew I should have used my new ability to lie.

"What a shame, you must let them serve you. It won't do to have your body untended. We can't afford distractions. They know well how to serve a warrior; you must encourage them to do it." She turned Syl's face from side to side and watched his eyes spark with anger.

"Don't worry, Kharis, I plan on being well-tended once we return from our ride.

"Remember they enjoy pain; it pleases them. A healthy dose of pain doled out during your pleasure heightens their orgasms and helps their seed settle your womb. It's a proven breeding strategy. Our birthrate increased after we began employing it," She pulled Syl's hair back, arching his neck away from her, and my hands itched to grab my sword.

Goddess, how could a place be so broken.

"Of course, my Queen," I said, swallowing the bile that rose in my throat. I tilted my head to him, kissing his lips lightly. I infused my kiss with warmth and felt him relax. "Allow me to dress, and I'll meet you for breakfast. Perhaps I'll have them attend me quickly, so the ride is more relaxed," I whispered against his lips.

"Excellent idea. They are skilled. It won't delay our departure. Do not allow them release as punishment for not tending to you last night. Let them think about it. They know their duties and likely didn't offer. She picked up the bloody, discarded whip and hummed appreciatively over it. "You fit so nicely here, Teagan, your work at his back put many lesser warriors to shame. Taking the whip, she brought it down on Syl's back, striking him expertly and efficiently again and again, then she moved to Kar. Before she left, every man in my Trio bled by her hand.

I sobbed at their feet when the door closed behind Kharis. I hoped to save them from this, and this was my punishment, not theirs. This was my punishment for stopping her last night.

The sound of Syl's first shocked whimper went through my heart like a blade. I could do nothing to help him with the pain, and it would be that much worse as his wounds were fresh. I fucking hated this place and these people.

Men were stronger physically, and I had no doubt they had at least a rudimentary knowledge of weapons; why did they not rise against this strange tyranny? But I knew the answer. The Queen told me herself. She cautioned me against using pronouns lest they get the idea they were people.

The men had grown up in this life, and it was normal for them. Maybe pain was comfort because they understood it. They knew nothing else.

If it were, indeed, my path to free this place, then that would have to change. Somehow, these men must see that they were men. Did I want them to rise and upend the scales? No. I wanted the scale balanced — light to dark, male to female, pleasure to pain. The world needs balance in all things.

I touched them, giving the last of my strength toward relief from their pain. I spread my arms and hugged them to me, sad that my decision brought this upon them. Initially, their bodies were stiff, but as my warmth shifted to them, leaving me cold, they softened and held me back.

A sense of camaraderie grew between us. We were in this together. It was us against this Goddess damned world, like it or not. Lyrolas had said that this was their last chance; the Queen had said they were challenging. If I failed with them, I sensed they would forfeit their lives as if they were untrainable beasts. No one said it in words, but I saw it in the Queen's eyes.

But they were not beasts. They were men, and if they didn't see it, I would make them. Swiping at my eyes, I pulled away from them.

"I apologize. My actions did this, and words cannot express how sorry I am for your pain. Forgive me." I grasped their hands in mine and bowed at their feet.

I heard their soft gasps and felt their surprise at my words.

"Should we tend you, my lady?" Kar's words were choked, and his voice strained. He spoke so sparingly that it was a surprise to hear them.

"Uh. No, Thalakar," I said, feeling his fear at my use of his name. My heart hardened against every warrior who had ever touched this quiet man before me. Hearing one's name should never cause fear. I smiled up at them all through tear-soaked lashes. "No. I don't need tending. I need men. Strong men who know their value, you are more than beatings and pain. Understand that." Sniffling, I rose to dress. Enough time had passed that the Queen would think I did as she commanded.

"Will you be okay here?" I asked, throwing on riding pants and buttoning my shirt.

"Yes, we will have meals in the slaves' hall and return immediately after. It's fine…Teagan," Syl said, and my face erupted in a smile.

My name sounded good on his tongue. "Very well, I'll ride with haste." I smiled at them again, then closed the door behind me.

Chapter Eight

Syl'ta

We stood staring at one another long after our wild-eyed mistress left. "Something is happening here, and I'm not sure I can begin to understand it," I broke the silence, then moved to start picking up her quarters. Our quarters, now, I supposed.

"What's happening is that she is going to get us killed," Lyros growled, snatching up items of clothing and placing them on hangers in the closet.

"We've worked hard at getting ourselves killed for longer than she's been Eruhini. She's merely going to speed up the process," I said, quickly clearing my section of the sitting area.

"You've done a good job, Syl. Not we. You." Kar threw a shirt at me, and I caught it.

"We've all contributed, Kar. Don't play the victim now," I said, tilting my head back in a laugh, causing the lash marks on my back to stretch. A groan slipped my lips before I could stop it. "How did she take the pain away?"

"Magic. You heard her. She is from the Light Court. Those lands overflow with it," he said, running his hands through his black hair.

"Magic?" I asked, pinning his black eyes with mine.

"Yes. There was a Trio of men taken from there decades ago. The tales they told were outlandish, but magic was at the heart of them all."

"And you believe that?" Lyros asked, turning to face us.

"She walked into a mirror and came back. The glass was unbreakable, despite our best efforts. She used a lash expertly on your back, and not one of us felt pain from it. Your back is beautifully marked, and yet there was no sting. When the Queen wielded the whip, we all felt it, yet our dark Mistress took the discomfort away with a kiss. If not magic, then what?" Kar said, talking as he worked.

"We're going to die," Lyros' mater of fact statement was not wrong.

"We were going to die anyway; maybe we can enjoy some of the time we have left," I said with a sigh.

Over the years, I tried to spread dissent through the ranks of the slaves. I was a natural-born leader and succeeded in showing the other men that what we suffered was not normal. My grandfather was once King of this place. He ruled side by side with my grandmother. Still, my sister was ambitious from the beginning. She overthrew him, killing them both in the process of staging a coup. She let our mother live as she did not oppose Kharis's rule.

She only killed her after I was born. My mother refused to allow me to go to the slave pens when I weaned from her breast. Having a son made her see the error of her oldest daughter's ways. Funny that losing her younger girls to the sword the oldest held wasn't what made her question the status quo. My birth did that.

A mother's love can change many things, but it couldn't change her fate or mine.

I went to the pens with my mother's blood on my skin, but Kharis, in some backhanded show of remorse, visited me and took an interest in my rearing. An odd affection sprang from her that I can only surmise meant she missed her mother.

I missed her too.

"Do you remember the time you put Troll lice on Ang'ali' s pillow?" I asked Kar, laughing at the memory.

"She scratched for weeks before she thought to tell us to change her sheets," I laughed back.

"Then Mori, she didn't deserve that worm you fed her, but it was funny all the same," Lyro added, catching my eye. His gray ones twinkled with devious delight.

He was right; she hadn't deserved it, but I saw the opportunity and took it.

"It hasn't always been bad, just mostly," he finished, and the light moment passed.

With three of us working, our quarters were clean and organized in a short time. Afterward, we made our way to the slaves' dining hall for lunch. We are not supposed to travel unescorted, but as Teagan's quarters lay in the rear of the palace where no one went, I had not thought to mention it. We slipped in unnoticed, easing into the food line so as not to attract attention.

Warriors lined the walls watching, but they rarely interfered. Only if there was a fight did they approach us. The hall and the exercise yard were areas we could whisper and plan unnoticed.

We ate in silence, catching the looks from surrounding Trios. They would think that our new mistress caused these wounds; only a few experienced men would recognize the intricate pattern the Queen places.

We held our heads high and ignored the glances and whispers that raced like wildfires. Let them think what they wanted; we would do nothing to defend Teagan. Should word of her mercy get out, it would cause trouble on many fronts. Let them think she was irredeemable, just like the rest.

We ate our fill and were headed to our rooms when I felt a hand on my shoulder. I turned into the angry face of Hel'r, the Queen's favorite tender. She doesn't have one Trio; she has many. She keeps pets in her quarters and makes use of the pens regularly. Our relationship is not as widely known as one might think. From time to time, it becomes common knowledge that I am her brother, then seems to be forgotten again by the wheel's next turn.

"Why you, Syl'ta? What did that exotic beauty see in your sad, little Trio?" He said, glancing at my crotch at the word little.

"What can I say, Hel'r? She must have *felt* something she liked," I winked at him and moved to pass.

He glared at my back. He would recognize those marks and be envious since not all men hated their predicament. Hel'r loved the Queen's punishments, and that's what made him her favorite. He took every bit of sadism she gave and begged for more, but she never took him into her rooms to make a pet of him. He was bitter, and everyone knew it; he would take it as an insult that all our backs were marked with the attention he felt should be reserved for him.

He grabbed my shoulder, whipping me around to face him. His eyes were hard, and his face lined with anger. "Why you? Why is it always you, Syl'ta? I want to know what sway you have. You should have died long ago, with all you cause is trouble."

Lyros moved to grab me before I could advance on my sister's favorite whipping boy and pulled me back. "Maybe I'm just that much better than you, Hel'r. I'm sure you know what I mean," I said, licking my lips suggestively.

He swung at me, and I ducked, putting my shoulder into his gut and taking him down to the ground with my mass. Shouts erupted around us, and he landed a lucky punch, bloodying my lip. I got in several hits of my own before the guards rushed in, pulling us apart.

They dragged us to the holding cells in the pit of the palace, and I instantly regretted letting him bait me. I knew. I knew what it meant. Slaves often fought in the pens' relative privacy and were ignored, but not publicly in full view of the guards.

"I think you've finally done it," the guard said, pushing me to my knees. My brothers landed next to me in a heap, bloodied from the beating the guards gave them.

Kar turned his back to me as the barred door slammed shut. "Why? Why Syl'ta?" His sigh was so deep it ended in a sob.

"Don't say anything; not this time," Lyros paced the wall furthest from me, a low growl escaping his lips.

They were right. I had done it this time. I scrambled, putting my back against the cold stone wall, waiting for the Queen to get back and decide to take my head, but only after our mistress paid for my crimes.

Chapter Nine

Teagan

I leaned down, pretending to lace my boots tighter. Taking advantage of the commotion as warriors prepared to ride out, I placed my hands on the cold ground. Summer is brief in Eregion. A warm sun and soft breeze last weeks, not months. Already snow flurried around us, and the Eregion version of fall set in. There was only one season in this frozen place. Aside from a few short weeks that would be spring anywhere else, there was only winter.

At this elevation, coniferous trees and small bushes were the only vegetation that grew. Vast highland plains with sparse, quick growing grasses that were harvested during the warm weeks and used to feed livestock during the long, cold months that followed. As with everything here, the animals were hardy and used to getting by with much less.

I let heat and power from the earth that was not yet buried deep within the snow travel through my tattoos, and I felt rejuvenated.

There is beauty in the stark, cold face of winter. It's not an empty thing at all. It's as if the earth sighs as she rests, and winter is the result. Winter is truth, for nothing can hide. Like an old woman who has lost the plump blush of youth, there is beauty and honesty in her bones.

"Mount up," The Queen cried as she pulled her sword from its sheath and reined her white mare to stand. "Second Blade with me," she shouted, and I scurried into my saddle, pulling my mare beside hers.

Every Fae that saw her wondered about Ari's mare, Solas. She was so out of place in Talamh na Sithe with her pure white coat, long, tall body, black eyes, and delicate face. Now I knew from where she came. Whether she was a gift from Queen to Queen or an escapee through the land of Trolls, Solas belonged here.

My mare was slightly taller than Ari's, and her deep, black eyes were kind. No white showed in them when I pulled her around and kicked her into a run to follow Kharis. The others pounded behind us in a cacophony of horses' hooves.

I knew nothing of our mission; I had not been briefed. I only knew that we rode to a neighboring village under the Queen's rule. As I had not yet been out of the city proper, I did not know what to expect.

What I did not expect were quaint rows of houses lining a wide, slow-moving river. Women dressed in brightly colored skirts walked through cobbled streets swept clear of snow. Men walked with them in groups or alone. They carried baskets and jugs; one carried a small deer draped across his shoulders. They froze when they saw us, bending their knee where they stood. I saw fear in their eyes before they lowered them to the ground, and I felt terrible. Never before had I been looked upon that way.

While the look of people in the city was still black, white, or silver, this town was colorful and bright. The men wore clothes instead of leather harnesses and skirts. They walked with the women. This could have been Talamh na Sithe, and I was more confused than ever.

The Queen wasted no time. "Have the wagons brought out and ready the infants," she spoke, scanning across the villagers.

"You're early, my Queen. We were not expecting you for another fortnight; the infants are still at the breast." A tall woman stepped forward, dressed in a deep green gown. Her long, silver hair lay braided around the side of her head, falling past the curve of her hip.

"Our arrival is fluid within the moon of this month. You should have weaned them in preparation." Queen Kharis watched as wagons laden with vegetables, fruit, caged livestock, flour, and sugar we brought around the corner by large, black mules. Her eyes were cold, and there was nothing behind them but death.

"Your wagons look light, Faldwyn." Kharis turned her glare to the woman.

"The warm season was short, Milady, as agreed; this is eighty percent of our harvest." The woman rose, inclining her head.

She saw me staring at her and caught my eye; confusion rippled across her face as she scanned my unusual coloration. Her eyes flickered nervously to Ang'ali as she kicked her horse and rode around the kneeling crowd, keeping her sword out. My horse shifted below me, uneasy. I felt the same way.

"Bring the infants; they will wean," Kharis said, her eyes sweeping the crowd.

Sobs broke out from women scattered through the crowd. Men grumbled, and angry eyes cast glances at the Queen, and as I was next to her, me. I didn't understand what was going on, but it most certainly wasn't right. Eighty percent of these peoples' harvest would leave them with little to survive on.

Women carried babies forward, and my stomach sank. If they intended to sacrifice these children, I would die here defending them. One hundred to one were terrible odds, but no child's blood would spill as long as I breathed.

"There are too many, My Queen. Can you not leave a few for us to raise?" Faldwyn stepped forward, her dark eyes beseeching.

"Do you wish to renegotiate your freedom?" Kharis said, her voice dripping with ice. She put her free hand on the hilt of her sheathed sword.

"No, Milady. I ask for a small concession as we had so many babes born this turn of the wheel," she said, her voice steady but her eyes shining with unshed tears.

"And the crown rewards you for your sacrifice. You live freely. You pay your tithe once yearly. We return those children unfit to serve. You live in peace, able to make your own daily choices. I will make no such concession, especially when your harvest carts are light. Should they be light again, I will increase the percentage I take. The city must be maintained." The Queen's hand relaxed when the other woman dropped her head.

"Bring them forward, and their sire as well."

I fought to keep my face neutral and cover the shock I felt. Faldwyn's eyes flicked to me again. I shifted in my saddle, struggling to show nothing.

Fourteen women stepped forward, clutching babes on hips or nestled in arms. I'd never seen an infant before and had no reference on how to age them, but most looked able to walk, if just barely. Some were smaller, round things with bright eyes and chubby cheeks; only two seemed so new as to appear wrinkled and still wet.

Kharis dismounted from her horse, handing the reins to me. She strolled the line of mothers, gazing into the faces of the babes they held. "These two may stay until next year," she said, touching the heads of the smallest bundles. "They are far too young for training." The rest will do. Excellent crop this year." She turned from them, walking toward a strong, muscular man with black hair and eyes so light blue they appeared white. "You did your job well." She leaned forward and placed a chaste kiss upon his lips. Stepping back, she pulled her sword and took his head before I could register the action.

My hand shot to my mouth, stifling a cry. Faldwyn looked at me again, tears streaming from her eyes. She held my gaze for a long moment before rushing to the dead man's side. She sobbed over his body, clutching his torso to her.

None of the other women reacted, and I knew that he had been hers, even though he fathered many children. He had belonged to her, and I wondered again about this place.

The Queen turned from them, holding my shocked stare. "Take them," she said, grabbing the nearest infant from its mother and tossing it to me.

Warriors around me dismounted, snatching babies from wailing mothers. Cries erupted from the townsfolk, and I chilled to the bone despite my warm cloak. I never saw such a look on anyone's face; it made my soul shrivel from the chill of it.

I caught the babe with one hand, pulling it tight to me. A cry so sharp came from the thing that I almost dropped it. I'd never seen a baby, let alone held one. My hands shook, and my eyes filled with tears when I looked down and saw the pitiful thing I held. It looked female. She was female.

They didn't just take the males, as I initially suspected; they took all the children. As gently as I could, I wrapped the baby in my fur cloak and placed it under my arm, thinking this could not be allowed to stand.

I looked across the sea of warriors and saw that the children were at least protected and warm; the bundles positioned as they readied to ride. Women dismounted, tied their horses to the carts the mules pulled, and started back the way we came. In silence, the townsfolk stared lifelessly as we moved out.

I watched as Kharis mounted her horse, pulling her reins from me. They said nothing as they turned their horses around, kicking them into a gallop. The sound of wailing infants and mothers shattered the air around me.

I hesitated for a moment, wheeling my horse in a circle one-handed, I caught Faldwyn's eyes once more, and something important passed between us. I nodded my head once at her then kicked my horse into a gallop, following the others away. This battle would be fought, but it would not be fought today. I needed to understand what happened here first.

The others had slowed to surround the wagons, and I caught them quickly. Kharis rounded on me as I approached, blocking me from the caravan that continued without us.

"You hesitated. I saw it in your eyes," she said, leveling her cool gaze on me. The silence settled between us, and I knew I had to use words selectively.

"I didn't understand the situation," I answered, meeting her eyes. Her face was so blank that I glanced at her hand to see if it rested on her sword.

"I saw violence on your face, and it was not toward the villagers. Many warriors have died on their first visit to that village. You did better than most but worse than others. Explain yourself." She stood still as ice, her hand hovering above her blade.

I did not know if I could take her in a fight. I was not given the opportunity to be First Blade. She held that title and had not raised her sword to mine during testing.

As I sat on that mare surrounded by the beauty and honesty that is winter, I knew that blood would flow on the snow around us. Whether it was now or sometime in the future, we would see if I could be First Blade. I heard the slow approach of horses circling behind me, and I knew that day was not today.

I was not a coward, but death in the middle of the Eregion high plains would not serve that purpose if I were to change this place.

"I see violence on your face now, Teagan. Choose wisely." She sat on her horse, watching my face with cold appraisal.

"There are no children in Talamh na Sithe. I am taken aback by many things in that village but more so the children. I've never seen a baby, never observed a mother with a baby. The man I understand as they are of little value," I added, "I don't understand the children." I cocked my head and cleared my face of expression to mirror hers.

I jostled the bundle in my arms enough to draw her eye to it. The child had quieted during our ride but stirred now and let out a wail.

She laughed so loudly it echoed across the plains and off the mountain beyond. "Of course," she said. "Of course, I should have warned a barren Fae about the babies," She laughed again, riding to my side and side-stepping her mare to mine. "Give her to me." She reached expectantly.

Taking the baby, I held her between us, not letting her go. Kharis moved my cloak from the baby's face, exposing it. "Someday, she will be a warrior. She will ride with us to that village, just as many women did today, and she will hold the next generation of warriors to her breast and ride away. Just as the males are raised from weaning to be slaves, the females are raised to be warriors. They stay with us and learn. They cannot be taught to be leaders and warriors in that village. Only we can do that. She will go to an old warrior who can no longer ride, and she will grow strong and learn to fight.

"If she is too soft to hold a sword, she will go back and bear the next generation of babies we cull. A percentage of handpicked males go back at breeding age to keep the wheel turning. It is the way of it."

"There are a dozen such villages across this land that live in peace and prosperity. We leave them alone. Their men are free. They can make their own choices and be independent until the day, once yearly, we come and collect our due.

"They may mate with whomever they choose, but the children must come from one man chosen by the village to be their sire. He is killed at the end of his cycle so that inbreeding is limited. This is the price of their freedom, and it works well for everyone involved." She smiled at me so sweetly and covered the baby's face, pushing her back to me.

"That makes perfect sense, Kharis," I said, smiling back even while I seethed on the inside. It was no better than what Aramea did. If anything, it was worse. Those people have no choice, not really. This was not freedom. None of it. I clutched one of the last living vestiges of the man who gave his life for those he loved closer to me, making her a silent vow to do better by them all.

"I'm glad you see it that way, Teagan, your life here will be long. Many new warriors struggle with the concepts that are the foundation of this land. More than you can imagine, die during that particular test of loyalty. Despite your initial hesitation, you did well. Come, let us join the others." She tapped the sides of her mare, urging her on, and I did the same. We were back at the wagons within moments.

Ang'ali glared as the Queen and I approached. Her hot eyes found mine, and I knew she would be a problem. The Queen just smiled and shook her head like we were errant teens. "You will adjust; I have no fear. You are a warrior at heart and fit perfectly among your sisters," Kharis said, moving to the front of the lines.

I followed, wanting to keep her close. Ang'ali moved to the opposite side of the Queen, and we rode three abreast back into the city.

Due to the wagons, the pace was slow. The sun sank low on the horizon as we neared the walls. The gates opened, and riders rode swiftly through them.

"I would speak to you, Kharis." A rider named Pameline slid to a stop in front of us while others went to take the wagons and the bundled babies from our arms.

I knew Pameline reasonably well as we often trained together and got along enough that I thought we might be friends. She cut her dark eyes at me, shifted in her saddle, and refused to meet my eyes. My stomach sank. Something was wrong.

"Speak freely, Pameline," Kharis said.

"Teagan's Trio are imprisoned. The troublesome one attacked one of your slaves." Pameline scrunched her eyebrows again, casting another glance my way.

"Which slave?" Kharis asked, her voice sharp with concern.

"The one called Hel'r," the warrior answered.

"Oh," the Queen said with a relieved sigh and soft shake of her head. "Not even a full day, and you will pay the price for your Trio's actions. I warned you to choose wisely. There's nothing to be done for it now, I suppose. Show her to the chains, Pameline; I will pass judgment shortly," sighing again; she rode away.

"What is the meaning of this?" I asked as Pameline rode next to me, taking my reins.

"That Trio will get you killed, Teagan. Why didn't you choose another? Any other would have been better. You have a way of finding trouble. Most girls lay low a bit and learn the lay of the land. Not you. No. You've got to waltz in here, beat the others at their best games, and then pick the worst possible slave group to serve you. Ugh," she finished.

I almost laughed. Almost. "First of all, I didn't waltz in here; a troll dragged me. Second of all, I had no idea about my Trio; I just felt a spark with them."

"Well, sparks lead to fire, and now you're going to get burned," she said, looking around quickly. She led me away from the others toward the palace courtyard. No one followed.

"What do you mean?" I asked, knowing the answer.

"One of your men started a fight this morning. Everyone knows they fight from time to time, but he did it in front of guards, and you will be whipped for it." She stopped, watching my face.

She called them men, not slaves. I filed that away for future reference. She was like me, not from this place, and maybe an ally could be made of her.

I sighed, dropping my head back in silent prayer to my Goddess. I had known this was a possibility. During my orientation, they taught that warriors faced the consequences for their slave's actions. They even taught what crimes lead to which punishments. That's why I never wanted a Trio. I can barely keep my actions from getting me killed. Now, somehow, I had to assure theirs were appropriate too.

This place sucked.

"So, now what?" I asked with a sigh, opening my eyes to catch her staring.

"You're very calm," she responded, scrunching her eyebrows together.

"Can I change it?" I asked.

"Maybe," she said, her gaze soft and searching.

"What do you mean?" I asked, narrowing my eyes.

"You can forsake them and pick others. You've only had them a day. I doubt she will rake you over the coals either way, but she may give you a choice." She watched me thoughtfully.

"No. They are not animals. They are no different from you and me. I chose them. Whatever the consequence, I will deal with it," I said, kicking my horse and walking past her.

"That is a fascinating concept. I wouldn't voice it too freely, Teagan. The women here do not view them as men." She moved her horse abreast of mine, and we walked them toward the courtyard. Better to get this over with quickly and move on.

"Do you feel that way?" I asked.

"No," she said, her voice so soft I strained to hear it.

"Then perhaps we can be friends," I said, not looking at her.

"I think I would like that, only being your friend might prove to be dangerous. Good thing I like danger," she laughed, kicking her horse into a trot. I followed, and together we went the rest of the way in silence.

In the courtyard, I dismounted, handing the reins off to a waiting slave. My men were on their knees, chained to one another by their wrists and ankles, their heads bowed to the ground. Syl'ta looked up, and I saw the sorrow in his eyes. The resigned slump of Kar's shoulders telegraphed his thoughts, and Lyros looked as if his soul had already fled. I gave a soft shake of my head in warning, and Syl'ta's face changed from sorrowful to concerned.

I stood at attention as the courtyard filled with warriors and slaves alike. Kharis moved out onto the balcony and wasted no time in reading the charges against me.

"Teagan Rilynoquar, you are here to answer for the charges against your Trio. The charge is disorderly conduct of a Trio and behavior unbecoming of a warrior. This is their fourth such charge and requires twelve lashes. As you are Fae, those lashes will be delivered with a cold iron chain so that you cannot heal them immediately and have time to consider your slaves' actions. How you deal with them afterward is your choice. As, by your admission, you have not mated with your Trio, and they have been in your care only a short time. A not guilty plea will free you from responsibility and allow you to start again. A guilty plea means you accept this punishment and responsibility for all their actions in the future. Understand that their infractions are cumulative over time. How do you plead?"

Without hesitation, I said, "Guilty."

Loud exclamations rose from the crowd. I guessed my response was unexpected.

"Very well then, remove your shirt and relinquish your arms to the chains," Kharis sighed, and I looked up, catching her speculative look.

Lyros had said this was their last chance. If I renounced them, I had no doubt that they would have died on this expanse of cold stone.

"I will not be chained. I accept punishment, but I will not be strung up while it is delivered," I said, cocking my brow at her.

She cocked her own in response, "You cannot move, Teagan; the chains are to help you with that."

"I will not move, Kharis," I said, standing straight and squaring my shoulders. "There is no pain in acceptance." I walked past my men, placing a kiss on each of their heads, then walked briskly to the wall.

The quiet intake of breath told me that the last bit was unorthodox, but I cared not one bit. I would change this place, and it would start today.

"Teagan's Trio, rise and see what your actions have wrought," The Queen said, turning to them.

She looked disappointed. It was hard to tell if it was because they caused this, or she had been denied the opportunity to end them finally. "May you consider this the next time you break the rules, though I doubt you care one bit. Trolls have more awareness of self; of this, I am sure."

At the wall, I stripped. Not just my shirt, but all of it. It was a pivotal moment. The significance of it settled in my bones, and I knew whatever happened was right.

The Queen always wanted my tattoos hidden, and I bet that many here did not know I had them. There was a reason for that. Those that considered men slaves and nothing more would think my tattoos made me something lesser.

Those warrior women who had an attachment, affection, or kind thoughts about their Trios might see this differently. Seeing me marked in this fashion might make the tattooed men seem more Erhuhini and less like animals.

I dropped my pants and my boots, kicking them into the pile of clothes, and stood bare to them all. Part of this was selfish, too; I wanted to make a point, and to make a point, I needed to be strong. I am strong, I didn't doubt that, but twelve lashes with an iron chain might be more than I could bear.

Cold Iron is a Fae's worst weakness, and I could not afford to be weak. The Queen knew it would make me heal slower, but she didn't seem to realize I had magic and that Cold Iron would take it from me. Pameline would not know any of this and would do her job as all warriors do: well.

A sharp gasp went up from the crowd as I showed all my skin in silence. I braced my arms at the wall and let my tattoos harness the power and heat from the ground beneath the stones until my skin tingled with it. I waited.

Pameline came, wielding the chain. I caught the faintest tremor in her hands from the corner of my eyes. "Do your job, friend, and worry not, for that is all it is," I said.

The first slap of the chain was tentative and slow. The second, not so much. I felt each sting as Pameline worked my back. It hurt. It hurt very much. Had power not been coursing up and down my tattoos, it would have been too much. As it was, I stood unflinching but just barely.

With each strike, the chain wrapped around my side, gripping the flesh on my breasts or belly, ripping it away. I kept my back and shoulders straight. I would not bow to them at this moment.

Blood trickled down and stung the marks as the iron slowly poisoned me. Much of that poison the stones took, but not all. I felt lightheaded and forced it away. In the privacy of my quarters, I would be weak, but not here.

On the eighth strike, the crowd gasped as the iron sank through my back and exposed bone. On the tenth, When Pameline chose to spare my back and strike my hips, the crowd grew motionless. The silence was tense, and as the chain wrapped around my ample backside and gripped the flesh on the front, more than one voice shouted out against the next strike.

The last strike wrapped the chain so tightly into the wound that Pameline had to pull it out with her fingers. Once free of the thin iron chain, I turned to face those gathered and let them see the results of my punishment. Maybe they knew Iron would hurt me, but they had surely not known it would mark me as it did- unless they had and meant to scar me. Steam rose from the wounds in the cold air as the touch of iron continued to scorch the flesh below. I stood naked, bloody, and still as they took it all in.

Iron should have leached my strange magic, but it did not. My tattoos throbbed with life as they took some of my pain and gave me the strength to stand.

The festive atmosphere had changed to pensive and had turned to anger as my blood ran steaming onto my feet and into the stones below.

Turning again so that my back was visible, I reached for clothes, draped them over my arm, and walked naked to my men.

"Release them," I said to the guard that held their chains. She looked up at the Queen for confirmation and, at her nod, released the Trio. I nodded once at the Queen, then walked with my men to the doors of the Palace, leaving bloody footprints in my wake.

Chapter Ten

Kar

If there were tears left in my soul, I would have cried them for our Mistress. I have witnessed many a beating of many a warrior, but I had never seen anything like this.

They meant to ruin her.

But she ruined their ruination with her strength. How does one so small contain so much? She walked with her destroyed back straight. It was trying to heal as I stared at it, but the poison in the chain stopped the magic she holds.

She said nothing as she walked, her bloody feet slapping on the marble floors as she went, trails of smoking blood marring its polished white perfection.

What manner of creature is she?

At the door to our rooms, she faltered, and Lyros scooped her up. She whined; it was the first and only noise she made during this ordeal as her body came into contact with his. We rushed through, closing it behind us. Lyros laid her on the bed and hurried to get cloths to clean her wounds. The skin of her face was burning hot, and her eyes did not open when I touched her.

"What now?" I asked, snapping my eyes to Syl'ta. "She's dying."

"She will not die, my child." The woman that stepped from the mirror was small. Very small. She had the pale skin and silver hair of a warrior woman, but her eyes were a purple so light as to be unnatural.

Her skin softly glowed, and peace rolled from her, causing me to drop to my knees. She was from this place but not. Lyros and Syl'ta dropped as well.

"Rise, Gentle Men. Bring Teagan and follow me." She turned in a swish of purple skirts and moved to the mirror. Teagan had gone into the thing and said she would explain but had not gotten the chance.

I grabbed her to me and ran for the mirror. Her skin slipped against mine and came off in pieces. Her temperature was so high it could not be survivable. Still, I followed the silver lady through the mirror as some new feeling slipped beyond the stone walls in my soul and took root. Faith.

This woman said Teagan would not die, and I believed her.

I slid through the mirror and felt nothing. I heard my brothers behind us, their feet pounding on the loamy soil beneath their feet. The purple and silver flash led me past glorious flowers and lush plants that do not grow in Eregion. I wondered if we had jumped worlds. I've heard of such things. Maybe this woman was taking us to Talamh na Sithe.

Rich, floral scents assaulted my nose, and soft greenery caressed my skin as I flew with our broken warrior down a path I could only hope did not lead to death. At the end of the trail, I stopped. Male bodies hit my back, but I stood my ground under their weight.

Beyond me stretched a grassy plain and large lake. Purple mountains rose in the distance, and animals I'd never seen before grazed together on the lush grass. I walked forward on bare feet, Teagan's body limp in my arms.

Ahead of me, the purple lady beckoned, "Place her in the water, and I will explain while she rests and heals."

This new faith bid me do as she said. I knew her. How I did not know, but I did. I walked forward into the water until warm water surrounded us.

"Join Thalakar," she said, turning to Lyros and Syl'ta.

"How do you know us?" Syl'ta demanded, crossing his arms.

"Stop, Syl'ta. You've done enough for one day," Lyros snapped at Syl. They stood facing one another with a threat of violence between them. I did not know who this woman was, but violence brought us here, and I feared it would also get us expelled.

"Stop. Both of you," I said. "Come into the water." I looked around as it turned pink with blood and hoped the lady did not lie. Teagan felt dead in my arms. She did not move, and if she breathed, I could not tell.

My brothers took in the scene before them and silently joined me, surrounding the wounded warrior in my arms. Syl'ta cupped water over the exposed parts of her, and we watched as bloody water ran in rivulets through the channels of her marked, naked skin. We watched as it slowly knit together.

The silver lady stood on the bank watching us. Her gown moved about her in a way that made it look like mist and not fabric at all. "Lyrolas, Syl'ta, and Thalakar, you may call me Dani. I am a friend to Teagan and Mother to you all. Look into your hearts and feel the truth of my words."

We did. Warm water embraced us while a soft, sweet breeze surrounded us, and I knew we were home. I opened my eyes and saw her smiling at me.

"I don't believe you," Lyros said.

Of course, he did.

"Lyros, shut up," I demanded.

"Lyros," the little woman said. "All your life, you have felt split in two. You've been disjointed and disconnected; have you not? You have felt as if you were missing a piece of your soul." She turned her lovely gaze to my brother, and when he shrank under it, I knew she spoke the truth.

"How did you know?" he whispered, not with reverence but with fear.

"Because I made you." She snapped her fingers, and where a man once stood, a wolf swam. It was the biggest wolf I ever saw. His fur was white, and Lyros's gray eyes looked from his face. I cried out and shielded Teagan from the beast that ate my brother and stole his eyes.

"Come," Dani walked forward, and the wolf went to her side, sitting at her heel. He was so large his head matched hers, and they looked eye to eye.

Something passed between them, and the wolf whined then lay down, crying into his paws. I looked at Teagan and found her lovely amber eyes were open. A soft smile lit her face, and I leaned down to kiss her lips. She opened her mouth, kissing me back.

I had never kissed. Slaves are not allowed to touch a warrior's lips with theirs. Only women can share that intimacy. Something came over me, and I kissed her harder. She responded, opening my mouth with her tongue and letting it dance with mine. I never danced before either, but it was wonderous, and I let it build.

A chuckle caused me to break the kiss, and I looked up to see Dani standing there watching with a twinkle in her eye. My arms dropped, and Teagan rolled from me to dive under the water and swim away like a sea creature.

"You're a Goddess," I said, feeling the truth of the answer settle in my soul.

"I'm The Goddess, dear, but don't get caught up in semantics. And call me Dani. I insist," she said, watching Teagan float and heal in the waters beyond us.

Her bloody marks were gone, leaving bumpy, raised scars. I hoped they would heal, too, as I hated for her to bear any mark brought on by our behavior. The wolf watched her swim as well, and I saw the sentience in his eyes. I watched as the wolf wandered off, sniffing everything.

I eased out of the water, giving the Goddess a wide berth. Syl followed, using me as a shield.

"You need not fear me," Dani said, turning to face us once we were clear of the lake's shore. "Had your people not forgotten me millennia ago, Lyros would have been changing his form since childhood. Kharis let you forget me so that she could be unrivaled. You know nothing else. Feel the power in the land. Let it make you free men.

Syl'ta cried out, dropping to his knees. I turned and watched in horror as blue flames licked over his tattoos, racing from his feet upward until they consumed him. From the fire came a silver fox, and I could not help but cry out in fear. I stumbled back against the Goddess and bounced forward to the silver fox with blue eyes and a black streak down its back.

"You are not a fox, Kar, and you are not a wolf," said The Goddess, taking a step toward me. I watched the fox run to the wolf, and together they rolled and played across the meadow's deep grass. I backed another step.

Her power rolled over me, and I dropped to my knees. Frozen in place, I watched as she walked to me. "Your power goes deeper than that, had your people embraced who they are from the beginning, you would have moved mountains and built a paradise. Someday you will rebuild your kingdom into something new, something better."

I cried out as golden flames took me, and molten, red liquid raced up my body. The ground trembled under me and liquified. I fought to rise, only to be pulled deeper into it. Struggling made it worse, and quickly I was buried alive.

I fought to breathe and dig my way up. Above me, excited yips and a long, low howl rent the silence, and I tried harder to reach them. Warmth spread through my limbs, and I felt the earth surround me in a soothing embrace, and I stilled.

All my life, I'd been a prisoner. All my life, I had been a slave. The energy that surrounded me began to move through me, and I calmed, breathing to fill my lungs. I breathed in deeply again and moved to straighten my limbs. As Teagan moved through the water like a sea creature, I swam through the earth. Never had I felt freer.

I felt sentience in the power around me, and I let it mark me however it wanted. I know my brothers care for me, but this feeling? This thing I felt? I didn't know it existed.

Without Teagan, it wouldn't have been possible.

Power coursed through me, and I accepted it; it equalized and balanced. I pushed off the ground below me, and the earth parted. I surfaced reborn.

I never knew my mother; only Syl'ta did. I knew my mother now; she was the ground beneath my feet and the power that moved my limbs. She was the breeze that ruffled my hair and the sun that lit my face. And I knew her.

"Teagan will never again feel the bite of Cold Iron, and you will forever have the power of your mother in your soul. Lyros is whole as he should have been from the beginning, and Syl'ta will move silent as air through your enemies," The Goddess said when I regained my ability to hear. Her look was the steel upon which battle plans are made. I stood naked before her, as the earth had stripped me of everything.

Teagan walked from the water like a slow, happy dream. Water streamed down her perfect skin, and her tattoos flashed silver. She shook her head, causing her curls to plump again as the water flew off. Peaked, light brown nipples pebbled at the temperature change. She was healed. "Thank you, Dani," she said, kneeling before the little Goddess.

"You take a beating that would have killed any other, and yet you thank me, Teagan. The world will bow to you someday," she said, resting her hand on Teagan's wild curls.

"I don't want the world to bow to me, Dani. I want Eregion to stand with me." Teagan rose, tilting her head so that the warm sun fully hit her face.

"And that is why you are destiny, Teagan. That is why." The Goddess turned and was gone. Not walking away, she was simply no longer there.

I turned to catch Teagan sinking to the ground. She stretched her limbs and let the sun warm her naked skin. I drank her in. Long lashes kissed her cheeks, and her chest rose and fell slowly, showing the soft curve of her rib as she breathed. Short, dark curls framed the dip of her sex between her hips' curves, and strong, muscular legs extended to pointed toes. She looked utterly relaxed and lethal as a blade lying there.

My cock stirred, and I looked down, stunned. I couldn't remember the last time my cock had risen of its own accord. Usually, I had to manipulate it. Yet now, it bounced against my stomach, and I stared at it in prepubescent wonder. I looked up and caught Teagan staring wide-eyed but unashamedly.

The bar all slaves are given at the onset of adulthood still pierced my cock front to back. The earth had not taken my nipple rings either, and I wondered what she thought of them. She smiled in what I hoped was an invitation, and I went to her.

I lay down, stretching my body alongside hers. She was hot. Her warm skin sizzled against mine, not in the way of illness, but in a manner I didn't fully understand. She rolled to me, feeling so perfect, tucked into my arms. Until that moment, I hadn't appreciated how good a woman could feel. Trained to give pleasure, that one small movement of her flesh pressed against mine gave me more joy than anything had.

The wolf and the fox came, sniffing at us. Lyros let out a soft whine, and I shooed him away. Let him be a man again and say his piece. Otherwise, I was ignoring him.

She tilted her lips, and I kissed her. Her hot tongue melded with mine, and her hands roamed my body. Her light touches tentative and exploring, and I worried. No female moved this way. I pulled from her and watched her face.

"What?" she said, trailing her fingers over the muscles in my chest and stopping at my nipple rings to slide her fingers over them. "Do these hurt? If they do, take them out," she said, her voice more breath than sound.

"They do not hurt, Mistress," I answered, clutching her hands in mine. "Have you…?" I asked, uncertain about how to finish the question.

"I'm not your Mistress, Thalakar. We are equals," she said, flashing her amber eyes at me even as her chin sunk deeper into my chest.

"My Lady, even in another land, we would not be equal. You are a Goddess," I said, with a soft chuckle, adding a nuzzle to the top of her head.

"You've met The Goddess," she countered. "I am no Goddess." She slid her hands from mine and began her gentle perusal of my flesh. "You're so beautiful," she said, and I couldn't help but bark a laugh.

"Me? I am beautiful? The sun doesn't shine if your face is hidden, My Lady. Now answer the question." Taking one hand, I tilted her chin upward to see her eyes better.

"No, I have not. I will not go to some female warrior to train for this. I will not. It's not my way. You will train me if training is needed, Kar," she said, bringing her lips to mine more firmly this time.

"Teagan. It's forbidden."

It was her turn to bark out a laugh. She tilted her head back and howled with laughter until she had to stop and catch her breath. "Thalakar, look around you. You are in The Goddess's paradise, she gave you the power of the earth, and you are holding a magically healed woman in your arms whilst a fox and wolf who were once men stalk us. Yet, you claim taking my virginity is forbidden?" She reached up and wiped away the little tears laughter causes.

I turned her to her back, and she inhaled sharply. "Perhaps you're right," I snarled at her neck.

In this land, I was a free man. In this land, I could do as I wished, and I very much wanted to sink my cock into the yielding warrior beneath me. "My piercing might hurt you," I said, giving her one last opportunity to turn me away.

"Does that steel rod please you?" she asked, and the look of pure innocence on her face melted the last of the wall around my heart.

"It does," I whispered, watching her face in wonder.

"Then wield it expertly," she said, trailing her tongue down my neck.

I bent to kiss her again, letting it build. She tasted sweet. We are rarely allowed dessert; to my limited knowledge, she tasted like cherries and fresh cream. It was a fight to pull my mouth from hers, and when I did, she groaned.

Trailing kisses down her neck and up again, I latched on to her earlobe and pulled it lightly. Her breath hitched, and her back arched. Even that small thing was new to her, and I wondered how she got so far in life with so little experience. I vowed to give her my best.

I slid my fingertips in the lightest touch possible down her sides so that gooseflesh raised and her nipples pulled impossibly tight. While I explored her body with my hand, I kissed across her collarbones and down the vee between her breasts, purposefully avoiding them. I raised her arms over her head, bringing kisses to the forgotten flesh under them, and she cried out.

Behind us, the fox yipped and growled, and I chuckled. Raising my hand, I pushed the power the Mother had given me, sending the fox rolling with a yip.

Teagan said at the ceremony that she would take Syl'ta first. She said it out of bravado and the need to say something to the Queen, who suggested she use me as I was bland and boring but pleasingly silent.

I was neither bland nor boring; I just never cared before. I did the minimum required to avoid punishment. Pleasing women who cared for nothing was like banging your head against the wall to create change. The exercise was futile and only earned you a headache.

Teagan's body under mine did things to me I didn't understand and made me feel something I had no reference for. I wanted nothing more than to please her, and that feeling turned the slave into a man.

I nuzzled her breast with the side of my face before latching onto her nipple and sucking the stiff peak, pulling it tight, only to let it go and grab it again. She cried out, grabbing the top of my head. "I can't," she said, "It's too much," she whimpered.

"Oh, Teagan. Teagan," I purred. "If you can still speak, it's not nearly enough. When I'm through, you will have no voice. Hush now." I silenced her with a kiss and thrilled when she went still under me.

I went to her other breast and pulled the nipple into my teeth, biting hard, but not too hard. There's a line between pleasure and pain, how well we slaves know it. I toed the line with her, sucking and biting her nipples until she whimpered.

I kept her arms pulled over her head and only let them go so that I could dip my hand between her legs and flick that tender bud until she begged me to stop while bucking her hips. She clutched my arms, trying to pull me from her and failing.

She scratched me with kitten claws, pulling at my hair to try to dislodge my mouth from her, then, with a sigh, she went limp. I slid my fingers up her bud, and a shiver went through her. I dipped my finger in the wetness pooling under her, using it to trace the tender skin around her opening, then moved a circle back up to the bud.

I completed the loop multiple times until it was hard, and she shook against me. Her eyes opened and locked onto mine.

She came, her amber eyes flaring wide and fluttering closed. A scream ripped from her, and she rose her hips to meet my hand. I plunged first one finger, then two into her and slid them in and out, making her cries sharper and more frantic. Sweat beaded on her forehead, and her eyes rolled back as the last of the orgasm clenched my fingers so tightly only wetness allowed them to move. I slipped in a third finger, and her body lost all tone; her arms limp at her sides. Her breathing shuddered before evening out.

It was the most beautiful thing I had ever seen. She was so fierce in her ways and so innocent in pleasure. Her face was an open book, and I had never seen anything more lovely.

All slaves are built for pleasure. Men who do not develop ample cocks are sent to the villages. You can teach the tongue, but the cock must be grown. I wanted her ready and needed her wet and open, or mine would cause her pain.

The piercing at the tip gave intense pleasure, but if not ready, it would just hurt. Kissing a line down her belly, I spread her limp legs wide enough to accommodate my body. I ran my tongue along the same path my finger traced earlier. Like a livewire, she moved. Her body tightened around me, legs coming over my back on instinct. I smiled into her sweetness, sucking her bud with varying pressure. I lapped at it with my tongue until her heels came to my head, holding me tight to her.

I applied pressure to her core with my thumb, freezing her orgasm at its apex, and shifted my position to cover her. I angled my cock and slid into her wet heat in one long, smooth stroke, releasing her core as I went. She screamed when I breached her and again when the bar hit her deepest parts. She begged me to stop. She said she was dying.

One cannot die from pleasure; I know that.

I did not stop. I pulled out and pushed back in. Her back curled in fixed ecstasy, her mouth froze in a wide O. The orgasm I held off took her, and she clamped around me with the strength of a fist, and I let out a startled umph.

Bringing my lips to hers, I kissed her mouth. She tangled her hands in my hair and clawed at the back of my head, kissing me hard and deep. I moved in her with inspiration, and her hips met mine in hard slaps.

She tangled her feet around my calves and held on as I gave her every pleasure I knew. I shifted her hips under me, grabbing a handful of her ass cheeks and forcing my piercing onto the spot that makes a woman see into forever. I used my cock to teach her what that spot was meant for.

When she cried out again, her voice hoarse from her passion, I covered her mouth. Of everything I have ever done to a woman, kissing is the most intimate. Your eyes can see into them, and your every breath is theirs. Her tongue fit mine to perfection, and her lovely cries filled the empty places in my soul.

So tight was she around my cock that the piercing pulled me taut, causing intense pleasure. It rolled down my spine, and my balls tightened to my body in anticipation. I held off, bringing her one more time before I allowed myself release.

A slave must remove his cock and spend his seed anywhere but inside his mistress unless she asks specifically for it. As a new man, I plunged deep inside Teagan and claimed her as mine, bathing her womb with the result of the most intense orgasm I have known.

It was a first for both of us.

Placing my forehead on hers, I fought to catch my breath and bring my heart to a regular rhythm. I kissed along Teagan's jaw and cheeks, finding her mouth again. She sighed under me, holding my eyes with hers. She smiled, slow and sated, and I knew I had not lied to her earlier. She looked well and truly pleased.

"Shall I carry you to the lake to ease any soreness?" I asked, brushing an errant curl from her face.

"No." Her voice was barely a croak, and she shook her head before continuing, "It's a pleasant sort of soreness; I think I'll hold on to it for a bit." She winked at me and moved to lay on her side.

Syl and Lyros had stopped pacing and settled on the edge of the lake, both of their gazes forlorn as they looked over at us. I smiled in their direction and pulled Teagan against my chest. "We should go. They may send someone to check on you. We've been here for hours," I said, sighing into her hair.

"There is no time here," she answered. "When we walk through the mirror, not a minute will have passed." She snuggled deeper into my arms.

"I'm sorry that you suffered for Syl's transgression," I said, finally.

"What happened?" she asked.

"One of Kharis's pets took a swing at Syl, and Syl tackled him. Hel'r baited Syl, and he bit, as he often does," I answered. It was the truth. Syl's hot temper had gotten more than one Mistress whipped.

"It shouldn't be this way. None of it. If you are to stay with me, then you must know I mean to change things. You are men, not slaves. I am a woman, not your master. This land is built on logs with no notches; it will fall eventually. I intend to shake the foundation a bit. If you'd rather not be involved, I understand." She looked at me with intelligent eyes, and I knew I was lost.

"Then, we change things together. Kharis is finished with us. We've done our fair share to exhaust her patience."

"You can't speak for them," she said, nodding in the direction of the irritated canines.

"I can. They are my brothers, and I know their hearts. In a land ruled by Kharis, we are already dead. Might as well go out with a bang." I pulled away reluctantly and moved to my feet, pulling Teagan with me. She winced as she stood, her cheeks heating to a beautiful shade of red.

Picking her up, I ran laughing to the lake and tossed her in. "Just in case you want a repeat performance, you should heal that soreness."

She sputtered and gasped at the surface, slapping the surface with her hands. "I'll get you for that!" she laughed, splashing water in my direction.

I dove in, and the fight was on. We played and splashed in the lake while the wolf and the fox made faces that showed just how embarrassed they were of my childish antics.

I couldn't have cared less.

For the first time in my life, I felt free.

Chapter Eleven

Teagan

If Thalakar were the boring and bland one, I'd meet certain death at the hands of the other two. There was nothing but fire in the black depths of his eyes when he looked at me.

There is a volcano in Talamh na Sithe that erupts from time to time, sending lava and ash into the sky. As the lava dumped into the lands beyond and cooled, it blackened on the surface. Underneath that black crust, red hot lava still boiled and teemed. That is the heart of fiery Thalakar. His dark looks and calm exterior do an excellent job of concealing the flames beneath.

I swam a lazy circle in the lake and let its healing powers soothe the soreness between my legs and elsewhere. Thalakar accomplished what eight Fae males failed in a fraction of the time I had been under their purview. I should thank him. Now I understood the fuss and why Airmed changed from a red-headed spitfire who could throw fireballs to a red-headed spitfire who could throw fireballs with a smile.

I wondered if I could throw fireballs. I would have to try that.

When I could kick my legs together and swim without feeling a twinge, I stepped from the water. Syl'ta, the fox, and Lyrolas, the wolf, waited at the mouth of the path leading to the mirror. Kar lounged against a tree, watching me in the lazy heated way men excel at, ankles crossed, arms loose at his sides.

I walked to him and extended my hand. He took it, and I pulled him to his feet. "I suppose we should go; we can't stay forever," I sighed.

"Why not?" he asked with a crooked smile.

"I think it goes against the whole 'change Eregion' thing we had in mind." I smiled back and led us to the path.

I wondered if Lyros and Syl could change back to men on their own or if they would be canines forever. That would be tough to explain. I'm sure there was a learning curve. Hopefully, they figured it out. They dropped beside us and matched their pace with mine.

"I don't care about Eregion. I care about you. I believed all women were devils without redeeming qualities until I met you. I fear Kharis will destroy you before we have a chance to find out what our lives could be." He stopped and gripped my shoulders, giving me the smallest of shakes.

"She will not. We will gather those around us who think and feel the way we do, and then we fight to defeat her and her supporters. With our combined magics, we are already ahead of this game, but we must wait and change the hearts and minds of the people around us, or all will be lost. A kingdom of four would be dull indeed," I said, watching understanding fill his dark eyes.

"You are wise," he said, kneeling before me.

"Stop that. Get up. It is the right thing to do, and we'll succeed if we garner others' support. Come; let us go." I took his hand and held it in mine.

We strolled the path looking at flowers as we passed. Tiny, brightly colored birds dove into them at speeds faster than the eye could see, and we marveled, even the canines. Syl tried to catch one with his teeth, and I laughed as the bird hovered in front of his snout, chittering angrily before dashing away.

Dani said that time passed once we left the meadow, so I hurried my steps in case, as Kar suggested, someone came to check on me. It wouldn't do to be caught stepping through the glass.

Lyros whined when we reached the mirror. We could see that the room beyond was empty, but it might not be for long. I stepped through and was nearly knocked to the ground by the large white wolf as he jumped in front of me.

Whether he was acting as guardian or afraid of being left behind, I can't say. In the air, he was a magnificent animal, but where his paws touched the ground, a man rose.

The same happened with Syl; I caught a flash of the black fur streaking his back, then the man stumbled forward as his momentum carried him. He caught himself on the wall and swore, turning with a flash of blue eyes in time to see Kar glide through the silver with the lithe grace of a cat.

"I was hoping you'd hop through as a toad," Lyros said, narrowing his eyes and glaring at Kar.

"Sorry, brother, no such luck," Kar replied, grabbing a towel and heading toward the bathing room.

A knock at the door stopped him. It stopped us all. With a flash, Lyros threw a dressing gown at me. Catching it, I wrapped it around myself moving to answer. I waited until the Trio had found coverings for themselves as well to open it. They had come through the glass in fur and landed in nothing.

I mourned that I hadn't the time to check them out more thoroughly as I cracked the door, placing my foot behind it so it could not open further.

"Teagan. Please. I didn't know that the lash would injure you so. Let me in; I need to see to your wounds." Pameline stood at the door, her face creased with concern.

"I'm fine, Pameline. There's no need. My Trio has seen to me already." I moved to close the door, and she placed her fingers in the crack so my only option was to leave the door open or close her fingers in it.

"Please, Teagan. I didn't know. I've never given so many lashes, and to fail would have caused another to step forward and deliver them. I tried my best to be kind; I had no idea the lash would flay you. Syl'ta," she said, turning her imploring gaze on him. "You know I am not cruel," she finished.

"You have always been fair, Pameline," he said, using her name and causing her to inhale sharply. I guessed we would see if my earlier impression of her rang true.

Could she be a friend? Better yet, could she be an ally?

"Then ask Teagan to let me in." Pameline removed her fingers from the door. I could close it and be done or open it and see where we stood.

I opened the door.

She rushed in, closed the door behind her, and leaned against it. "I brought salves to take the sting out and creams to help it scar faster. I can offer nothing else," she said, walking to me. She held her hands forward so I could see she was not armed. Her pockets bulged and clinked as glass bottles rattled with each step.

"Let me see your wounds, Teagan."

"That's unnecessary, Pameline." I countered, pulling my gown tighter.

"Show her," Kar said, moving to stand behind me. "Let her see."

I paused, took a deep breath, and opened the robe, letting it drop.

Her startled cry broke the silence.

She tried to say many things, but the only word that came out was, "How?"

"The Goddess healed me," I answered. "I could have healed the lashes on my own, but not the iron poisoning." I closed the dressing gown, belting it again.

"I don't. I don't understand." She moved to the settee and sank onto it.

I went to the sofa, my Trio followed. In front of another warrior, they should be on their knees, but they sat, surrounding me with quiet strength.

"Pameline, I am Daoine Sidhe, as are you. As is every Eruhini. We are The Goddess's people. I was born with magic that was weakened by a sick land, but your land is strong, and my magic returned. The tattoos bloomed on my skin the first time my bare feet touched Eregion soil."

"And that is where your healing power lies? The tattoos?" she asked.

"No, they are where all my power lies, Pameline," I said, catching her dark eyes with mine. I wasn't going to tell her anything more specific than that. Should she not be an ally but an enemy, I would give her no knowledge that could weaken me.

"If I am Daoine Sidhe, as you say, where is my magic?" she asked. "I have none." She sat back and took me in. Kar's hand rested idly on my back. Syl had reclined and placed his ankle on the opposite knee, and Lyros perched forward, hands clasped between his knees.

We were not the picture of Eregion normalcy, and I knew that. Pameline knew it too.

"Where is your homeland?" I asked. "You aren't from Eregion any more than I am." I leaned back into Kar and watched her eyes flicker between us.

"I am Gwyllion," she answered, her eyes finally resting on mine.

"Of course, you are; I should have known." I couldn't help the smile that spread across my face. Her large, almond-shaped eyes set wider apart than the average Fae and were topped with heavy brows. Sharply pointed ears poked from her thick, yellow hair. Erhu ears pointed as well, but subtly so.

She was large and heavily muscled. Where I had curves with my muscle, she was all muscle. I should have guessed her origin from the start. As one of The Eight, I took classes on everything, including ancestry and heritage. The Gwyllion are mentioned in our Origins story. They are a mysterious sister race from beyond the dark mountains.

"You are Daoine Sidhe, same as the Erhus, same as the Fae. Ask your Goddess where your power is, and perhaps you will find it," I said, gently.

"She's real? Not some tale?" she asked, leaning forward to match Lyros.

"She is real. I have seen her. We have all seen her," Syl'ta said, taking my free hand in his. He lifted his other hand, and blue flames raced up his arms, following the lines of his tattoos. My brothers and I are also Daoine Sidhe. We are men, not beasts. Things were not always as they are, Pameline. I don't remember those days, but I believe in them.

"You're going to unleash a storm, Teagan. If they can't chain you, they will kill you." She tilted her head to the ceiling and blinked rapidly. "You and any that stand with you."

"Then don't stand with me, but don't stand against me," I said.

She tilted her face back to mine and held my eyes. "It's a good thing I like storms, Teagan Rilynoquar, First Fist, Second Blade, and Third Anvil. You should work on bettering that last one." She winked at me. She was the First Anvil, she would know.

"Kharis will come. She sent me first, but she will follow. What are your plans?" She asked, pulling the salves from her pockets and setting them on the low table between us.

"I have none. Not yet," I said as a knock sounded on my door.

My Trio sank to their knees with a disgruntled sigh. Pameline stood, but I stayed seated. The door opened, and Kharis swept through, ringed by the two smaller females that often attended her.

"Teagan, are you well?" she asked, taking in the position of my men. It was obvious they had dropped from the sofa to their knees. The salves sat untouched. And Pameline shifted on her feet.

"Already healed, My Queen," I answered, knowing it would be impossible to hide it. Word would spread, and questions would be asked. "I was just complimenting Pameline on her use of the lash."

"Healed?" Kharis said, her eyes narrowing.

There would be no talk of sisterhood and Goddesses with Kharis. She was the problem. Her mind had changed this place all those years ago, and there would be no changing it. "I'm Fae, Kharis. I heal."

"That's wonderful to hear, Teagan," she said, recovering quickly. "I came to see if you changed your mind about this Trio. I can take them and issue you another so that this type of thing doesn't happen again. Surely you recognize your mistake in choosing them. It can be remedied." She walked to a tall backed chair that resembled a throne and sat, her attendants standing to either side of her.

"I'm rather fond of them already, Kharis. My decision stands." I wanted to touch them, but in touching them now, it cheapened them. They were not pets or possessions and had free will within these walls, as promised during our first conversation. Instead, I rested my hands in my lap to keep them still. "I like a bit of fire with my ice," I said with a wink.

"Then, you shall have it." She rose to her feet, and her attendants stepped back. "Come Pameline, leave Teagan to rest," she said, closing the door behind them as they left.

With a sigh, I sat back. "It will start now, plan, or no."

"What will start?" Lyros asked.

"The storm," Syl'ta and I answered simultaneously.

"Despite our time in the mirror, or perhaps because of it," he said, casting a dark glare at Kar. "It's been a long day. I, for one, think Teagan should rest. We all should rest."

"Syl's right," I said, watching as looks of astonishment swept their faces. "I'm going to clean off," I said, stealing the shower from Kar, who had headed there when the first knock sounded.

Leaving the door open, I adjusted the nozzles, still marveling that hot water shot from the walls on demand.

Stepping in, I turned my back to the water and picked up the bottle of a special mixture I used to keep my curls supple and tamed, massaging it into my hair.

"I'm drawn to you." I opened my eyes to see Lyros standing there, his fist clenched at his sides and his towel on the floor.

I stepped back, inviting him in. "I'm not shy, Lyros. I want to touch you, may I?" I asked, watching him tilt his head in thought.

"No one has asked me that before," he said. His accent deepened, and his face held questions.

The Eruhini language is hard and has edges sharper than any blade. It was similar enough that I learned it quickly, but when the accent deepens, it can be more challenging to understand.

"You can say no." I picked up the soap and began to sponge myself while he watched.

"I don't understand any of this," he said, moving deeper into the large stone shower.

"Neither do I. How can we? It's crazy," I said, dropping the sponge then moving to rinse the soap from my skin.

"Yes," he said.

He stepped to me and reached his hand to my face. Hooded gray eyes looked at me with confusion.

"How can I trust this? You could still follow Kharis," he said.

I threw my head back and laughed. "No, Lyrolas. The die is cast. I have faith in my Goddess, and if she wants the Eruhini people back, she will get them, by my sword, she will get them." I stepped into him and covered the hand touching my face with my own.

On my tiptoes, I reached his lips, kissing them. I trailed my fingers down his sides, feeling the bumps pleasure causes rise. I brought them up in slow, teasing motions. His breath caught, I slipped my tongue deeper into his mouth and tasted him. He was sweet, like one Ari's cakes; I dipped my tongue in and groaned at the feel of his velvet tongue on mine.

"Have you ever been pleased by a woman?" I asked, against his lips. His eyes narrowed on mine, and he pulled away.

"I've spent my seed. We all have," he said, once again looking confused.

"That's not what I mean, Lyros." I pushed him backward until the backs of his knees hit the stone bench.

He sat back, and I followed him down, settling between his thighs; my head came to his middle section. Leaning up, I ran my tongue down his neck and across his shoulder. I kissed the flesh at the base of his neck and trailed my kisses lower.

I took the ring piercing his nipple in my mouth and softly sucked it, causing his chest to rumble. Trailing my hands up his back, I licked over to the other nipple and sucked it harder, taking the ring in my teeth and pulling it carefully. Pressing in closer, I felt his cock rise against my stomach, and I gripped it in my hand, sliding up until I reached the bar at his crown. I pulled it ever so slightly, and he melted against me.

We had classes on sexuality. As the last eight females born, we were expected to please our mates and bear them children.

Somehow, despite generations of barrenness, we were blamed before we could even experience sex. I knew the ins and outs of a cock long before I ever saw one in person. I wondered if my Trios' training and mine were all that dissimilar.

I kissed lower and lower still, bringing my arms around his thighs and spreading them wide. He grabbed at my hair, trying to stop me. "You must stop, Teagan. Whatever it is you're going to do, don't. It's beyond the pale for you to touch me with your mouth," he said, frantically trying to move away from me.

"Stop fighting, Lyros," I chuckled at his alarm. "I've never done this, and I'd hate to bite you." I licked up the face of his cock before taking it into my mouth and scandalizing him. His squeal turned to a groan, and despite years of brainwashing, he did as a man should and sank his hands into my hair, letting out a pained sound as my teeth found his piercing and tugged it.

"Teagan," my name was breathy on his lips, and his hips rocked against me helplessly. I pulled my arm free and used it to hold his cock while he fucked my mouth.

He was like a man starved; he couldn't stop. His hips slammed into my face, and I liked it. I moaned around him, gripped his bar, nearly pulling it out, and he cried out in pleasure as I learned something about this Erhu man; he liked it rough. Whether by training or by nature, he liked it the hard way, and I found I did too.

I gripped the base of him to control his wild thrusts and pushed him down to the bench, retaking control. I slid my mouth and tongue over him until he shook with the force it took for him to sit still, and when he started bucking into me again, I let him.

Drool ran down his shaft, coating his balls, and I used it to slide my hand over them, pulling them hard. He roared as his seed erupted down my throat, and I groaned at the feel of it. He tried to pull away, but I used the strength in my muscles and my tattoos to hold him while I swallowed each hot, sweet spurt he gave.

When he was limp under me in every way, I rested my cheek on his sticky thigh and smiled into it.

"Mm," I said, pushing off him to stand. "You taste wonderful." I washed again and tended to my hair while he sat there, his head lolled to the side watching.

"I can't move," he said, and I laughed.

"You can move," I said, and he growled. "I give to you, and you receive. You give to me, and I receive. That is the way it should be, Lyros. That is what mates do, and that is what partners do. I left him with a smile on his slack face.

When I stepped from the shower, Syl'ta was there, holding a towel for me. I walked into it, and he picked me up, carrying me to the bed.

I had one moment to wonder what was going on before he buried himself deep inside of me. I cried out at the abruptness of it.

"I am not fearful, Teagan, and I am not shy," he said, rolling his hips against me. He was bigger than Kar, and his bar immediately found the spot that sent me howling with an arched back.

"So you're not, Syl," I said when I found my voice. "I'm not shy either. I've waited my whole life to experience this. Life is short, and I've missed too much already, I refuse to miss more. You must find pleasure in the beauty of lightning on a stormy day or find no pleasure at all. I choose pleasure." I reached up and pulled his mouth to mine, glorying in the feel of his cock in me.

I didn't care that I'd only known him a day. It didn't matter one bit. Having been in three homes with eleven men, I knew anything could happen. I was taking what I wanted with no regrets. Regrets are for those who are too afraid to live and too scared to die. I was neither.

He kissed me deeply, his tongue as hard and hot as the part of him piercing me to my core. He pulled out and slid in again, and the rod hit the Goddess's spot, forever known in my mind afterward as the 'G spot,' and I came, arching into him and clutching hard at his arms. I couldn't breathe or move as he slid home inside of me, each time manipulating that spot until I was limp.

When I thought I could take no more, he turned me to my belly and spread my legs wide. His hands kneaded the muscles of my legs up to the mounds of my ass. His thumb grazed that swollen, tender piece of flesh as he eased muscles I did not know were sore until I began to squirm and rise to his hands. He gripped the mounds hard and spread them, pulling me to my knees.

He entered me from behind, and I screamed, arching my back to get away from the immense pressure of him in my deepest parts. He gripped my hips and pulled out. I sighed, relaxing as the pressure eased, but the relief did not last long. He angled his hips and pushed into me again, taking my breath away. I closed my eyes against the feeling of fullness that threatened to overwhelm me. Syl was patient as he waited for my muscles to ease and my breathing to slow, and then he systematically tore me apart.

Lips caressed the back of my neck as Syl moved in me; I opened my eyes and found Lyros on his side, stretched across the bed. He brought his lips to mine, and I kissed him. It was slow at first. I couldn't get the timing of kissing him and being thrust into in at the same time quite right, but Lyros knew and took over, leaving me entirely at their combined mercies.

Deft fingers strummed my core while Syl slid in and out of me, each time his piercing hitting my cervix in the most delicious of ways. Kar leaned against the headboard watching as his brothers melted me into nothing between them. His dark eyes glittered on mine in unconcealed lust, and I wondered how many times these men performed some parody of these same actions with other women.

I cared for a moment. Just one. It left with the next thrust of Syl'ta's hips. I had no idea how old they were; they'd been slaves all those years. No doubt they had done many, many things. That was the way of it. Someday they would be free men, free to choose their paths. Did I hope they stayed with me? Maybe. At this moment of pure, perfect pleasure, pulled tight between two of them? Yes. Yes, I wanted them to stay with me, but today was based on my choice, tomorrow would be based on theirs.

Lyros rose to his knees and pulled me to his lips, taking the weight from my arms and holding me to his chest. Syl's thrusts were wild, deep, and shattering. Lyros took my cries into his mouth and kept his skilled fingers on the bundle of nerves screaming between my legs, and I came again, throwing my head back with a hoarse cry.

Lyros gripped my breasts in his hands to the point of pain and bit down my neck as I clamped onto Syl'ta so tightly I felt the details of the hard length pushed impossibly deep inside me.

He shuddered and groaned, lost his rhythm, and bathed me in hot fluids. He pulsed so forcefully I cried out again, sagging against Lyros.

Syl ran his hands down my spine as the last of our spasms faded. I heard the rapid rise of fall of his breathing behind me but could not have moved from him if I tried.

Together, they laid me gently on the bed. Kar pulled me to him and cradled me against his chest, kissing my face. He smelled like damp earth and sweet oxidation. I could smell myself on him, too, as he never got the shower he wanted. The smell was soothing. I felt the bed rise. It dipped again, and hot towels sponged me clean. A delicious sense of soreness settled inside of me, and I was asleep instantly, surrounded by the muscular bodies of my Trio.

Chapter Twelve

Lyros

Our Queen sleeps in the midst of us. Her lovely face flushed and slack, her mouth softly open. We've had countless women in every possible way, but none compared to her, not for any of us.

Eruhini warriors approach sex like they do everything else; it's a battle they must win. Yes, they want pleasure, but there's no softness in it, and they never yield themselves.

We would often end the night bloodied. They must teach this to one another before a warrior beds her slaves, for they are all the same. The only variance is their level of cruelty. At least this is our experience.

Teagan is nothing like that. Her muscular body was pliant softness and the way she melted under our touch like nothing we experienced before. Talamh na Sithe must be a truly different place. The telltale blush of her cheeks as she gave more to us in one day than we received in our entire lives spoke volumes about her innocence.

She did not belong here- she belonged anywhere else. This harsh land would extinguish the light and innocence in her as it does everything it touches. I leaned on my elbow and traced the lines of her face. She was beautiful and so alive, unlike anything I had seen before. Her dark skin radiated warmth, and I thought maybe, just maybe, she could melt the ice at the Eregion heart.

"We should spread rumors in the pens," Syl said, already trying to get her killed. Again. "Spread rumors of the Goddess who gives power and women who feel something in their hearts. If we do it carefully, with the right slaves, the avalanche will start, and no one will know the origin.

"Word will spread to the warriors from their slaves, and maybe a seed will root. No doubt, word spreads already that Teagan's wounds have healed. That speaks to a greater power. It's not a bad plan," Kar said, shocking me. He rarely agreed with Syl's wild plans.

"The Queen will catch on and cut her losses. Teagan won't be the first stolen one to pay the price for higher ideals," I said, tracing the line of muscles on Teagan's arms. She was strong, but I feared the Queen was stronger.

"No stolen one has ever had power like Teagan," Syl said.

"We don't even know what she can do. I don't think she does either," I whispered, meeting his blue eyes. Syl was brazen, always had been. As Kharis's brother, he was afforded leeway when others weren't, and he had bold ideas because of it. Kar and I paid the price for those ideas as we were Syl's brothers.

We loved him, that is true, but I didn't want Teagan to die for us.

"Then we find out, Lyros; this is our chance. If The Goddess says this will work, then it will work. Where did your faith go? You saw what she did. She gave us power we did not have." said Syl, placing a soft kiss on Teagan's forehead,

"And it's made you bold, Syl. What if she dies? What if we all die?" I answered, sliding closer to the heat source in our bed.

"Lyros," Kar started. "You heard Teagan. Life is short. This is the best opportunity we will ever have. If I'm to die anyway, I'd rather die fighting for freedom than die a slave," he finished, tracing a finger over the firm peak of her bare nipple. Her chest rose to his touch, seeking him out. It was not expected, this response she had, but I liked it.

I sighed, "I suppose you're right. It is her choice, though I know what she will choose. She's been charged by her Goddess, and I don't see her backing down. Not the way she stood and took a poisoned lash for slaves she barely knows." I pushed a wild curl from the corner of her mouth, and she sighed softly in her sleep, rolling into me and curling her knees upward.

"This Goddess of hers is now our Goddess. We've seen her. We can't help but believe," Kar said.

"I agree. I felt her power before we stepped into the mirror, and it felt right to me. I believe she is our Goddess and that

Kharis wanted us to forget. Forgetting our origins has made us weak. We've forgotten our worth," I said.

Kar eased in behind Teagan so that his body fit around hers, and she wiggled her round ass slightly to adjust perfectly to him. None of this was normal. "A man who forgets his worth depends on others to tell him what his value is. We are worthy of more," he said.

"We will do as Syl says and spread word in the pens of Teagan's magic and our Goddess. We must also compile a list of warriors who might lend their swords to the cause; not all of them are savages. Teagan will need all the blades she can get," Kar finished. Despite his dark silence, or maybe because of it, he has always been the wisest of us.

He listens where others speak and sees more than most.

We can fight. Most slaves know some methods of fighting. The three of us have held swords and sparred lightly with warriors for their training. Our muscle mass is higher than theirs by nature, and they've used several slaves for training in preparation to fight against races with warrior males. We will hone this and practice in the tunnels with the most trusted among us." Syl's blue eyes sparked with new fire. He was right. We were not weak; we were underestimated. Having been viewed as lesser for generations might work to our advantage.

"Then there is the magic," I said. We must learn to use it as well. As I watched you fuck Teagan, Kar, I tried to turn back into a man so I could drag you off of her, but it didn't work." His black eyes flashed, and I leaned over, punching him lightly on the arm, he hit me back, and soon we were fighting quietly around Teagan so as not to disturb her. "Stop," I wheezed. "You'll wake her." I felt light with laughter and couldn't remember the last time, if ever there was one, when I felt that way.

We settled around her warm body again. "We must practice, and so must she. There's no use having magic in a fight if we don't know how to do anything with it," I said.

"Right," the other two said.

Into the long hours of the night, we whispered plans. Teagan had strength, but we knew this place. We would be model slaves until we could align allies and count foes.

Teagan would never again suffer for our misdeeds, even though they were not misdeeds at all. We would be careful, and we would train. We would build an army to follow a worthy warrior into a new age.

The Queen would tolerate no influence contrary to hers, so we must work fast as secrets are impossible when words echo off the ice. We must be ready.

I stoked the fires when they burned low, and soon we stopped talking to enjoy the warmth of our newfound circumstances. The more I thought on it, the more I realized divine intervention brought these changes. The odds against

Teagan picking our Trio were high. The odds against Teagan being stolen and brought to Eregion even greater. This was planned. I believed.

Sometime during the darkest hours of the long winter's night, we slept. Forgetting that just a few days ago, we had been in the cold, cramped slave pens, and before that, on the floor of some already forgotten warrior's home.

Now we were men on a tall bed surrounding a glorious warrior strong in conviction and soft of heart. She had taken to us and accepted us as equals. She sought to free our brothers and stop the tyranny that was Kharis and her followers. It was a new day, and I, for one, was excited to see what it brought.

Chapter Thirteen

Syl'ta

For the first time since I was a babe, I slept in. We all did. It's untoward. We awoke to platters of bread, cheese, and meat on the sideboard and the sound of Teagan showering.

I smiled at the memory of last night. I had ruined Teagan's shower, and now I set out to destroy it again. Never would such a thought have occurred to me before.

"You're a scamp," she said when I sneaked up behind her to slide my hands over her hips.

"I can't help that you're gorgeous. You've bewitched me into placing my hands on you," I murmured against her ear.

"Is that so?" she asked as I pressed kisses down the side of her neck. She tilted her head, giving me better access.

"Yes. It's so. As much as I want this week with you, we need you to send us back to work early; we can't afford to let Kharis get the upper hand." I trailed my fingertips down her arms, bringing little bumps to her skin.

She turned in my arms, her face serious. "There is a dignitary from some undoubtedly horrible place coming today. Kharis is hosting a formal luncheon; we're all expected to attend," she said, draping her arms over my shoulders and taking a surreptitious glance down. And then another.

I wanted to joke and tell her that my eyes were higher, but I liked the cute way she was looking at my cock. "How did that fit in me yesterday?" she whispered, tilting her head to look at me from a different angle. Her curls brushed my shoulder as she continued her slow perusal of my body.

"It just does," I said. "It's magic." I chuckled, leaning in and capturing her mouth with mine. I found I liked kissing quite a lot. I couldn't stop my lips from seeking hers.

"Magic indeed," she said, taking her hand and grazing my pierced crown. She touched so gently that it was painful.

"We should shower quickly," I said, turning her around and soaping her back. I ran my hands lightly down her sides and up again until little bumps dotted her flesh. I used the pad of my thumb to trace the line of the vertebrae in her spine, and she let out a soft sigh.

Soaping my hands more, I found the tight spots in her back and massaged them until she leaned forward, bracing against the wall.

Leaning over to place my lips against her ear, "If we must be there, then we should go wake up the others."

"Or," she said, her voice holding a slight quiver. "We could stay here and skip it. It's our joining week. There should be no more required of us than that."

"I do agree, but," I let the words trail off and slipped my thumb into her, curling it around so I could rub that sensitive place deep inside her. "She may come for us, and that would be bad.

She sank her head onto her chest, and I slid my thumb out, replacing it with my cock. I slid into her inch by inch so that she could adjust to accommodate my size. When my balls hit the tops of her thighs, I slid out, feeling her wetness coat me. I rammed back into her, feeling the slap of my sack against her before easing out with excruciating slowness again.

She bent lower, changing the angle. I repeated the action until she was panting and writhing on me, the tightness of her walls tugging on the silver rod at the end of my cock. I fought to control my pace, for I wanted her to experience this feeling. Her body was limp, and her legs shook. Reaching around, I roughly pulled her nipples, rolling them in my fingers, and she shattered around me, bucking onto me with abandon. Her screams echoed off the shower walls, and I gripped her hips to keep her from falling as I slammed into her. When the only sounds she made were grunts and whimpers, I came, filling her tight, little body with the only thing I had to offer other than my soul. I could not help the roar that came from me as the final tug on my rod sent me over the edge.

I stood, breathing hard, watching the skin between Teagan's ribs pull tight as she tried to catch her breath too. I pushed her to the bench and sat her down before she fell.

"You boys are going to be the death of me, not this land, not this Queen. You. Boys," she smiled softly, tilting her head back and resting it on the shower wall.

I soaped her again, then myself, before I pulled her up and rinsed her off. With a sigh, she straightened, brought her lips to mine, and caught me in the colorful depths of her amber eyes. "Kharis told me to choose wisely, and I did, Syl'ta," she said, bringing her hand up to cradle my cheek.

This thing between us was foreign to me. Teagan was foreign to me. Yet, she felt like home in the few short days I had been with her. She spoke of free men and choice, but I didn't want to be free, not from her. I loved Eregion. I didn't want to be free from her, either. I would stand with my home and with my warrior and fight whatever came. I did not want to lose either of them. But fate is fickle, and time would tell if I chose wisely or not. As I held the multifaceted green depths of Teagan's eyes, I believed I, too, had chosen well.

I got out first, handing Teagan a towel. She used it to dry off and then hung it on the wall, walking into our bedroom naked. Kar's hungry eyes seared onto her flesh when she walked to the armoire to choose clothing for the day, and Lyros arched a silver eyebrow at me and gave a slow wink and knowing smile.

I gave him a sly thumbs up then pantomimed running my hands down the bubble of her ass.

"Ah-hem, gentlemen," she laughed, catching me. If you plan to come with me this morning, and you should, for appearance's sake, stop congratulating your brother on his sexual prowess and get out of bed." I pulled blankets back, exposing their tattooed skin.

Kar shot me a dark look, and Lyros waggled his eyebrows before they both rose, their cocks straining in Teagan's direction.

"Dear Goddess," she said, tossing her head back and laughing, but not before she gave both men a long look of desire. "If I survive until you are bored with me, it will be a miracle."

"I doubt that will happen, my lady. Eregion slaves are bred for stamina and to be ever ready. We will never tire of you," Lyros flipped his hair over his shoulder, showing off his well-defined chest, and Teagan flushed, reaching for him.

I stepped between them and thought they would fight me to get to one another. "We must go. These events are political, and we need to be there. You know that."

"Said the brother who's orgasmic roar awoke me from sleep," Lyros punched Syl hard on the bicep.

Syl's eyebrows hit his hairline, and I palmed my face as they strained to fight each other like a couple of pissed off Luisine Badgers.

Or teenagers.

Once, I read a book that showcased human teenage boy behavior. It was not dissimilar.

"Gentlemen, please," I said, my shoulders shaking with repressed laughter. No wonder this Trio had gotten into so much trouble. They certainly displayed behavior unbecoming of an Eregion slave; however, I had never wanted Eregion slaves, and their behavior was just fine with me.

We walked into the Hall only a tad late. I led the way, Syl immediately behind me. Lyros and Kar walked a step behind him, one to his right, the other to his left.

Dressed in studded leather war skirts, their bare, oiled chests gleaming under leather studded straps that crisscrossed their chiseled chests, they were breathtaking. As we marched in step into the room, backs straight and heads high, all eyes locked on us.

I had chosen a white, diaphanous dress that left my left shoulder bare and draped my body to show my curves but not restrict my movements. A thin strap of silk covered my hips, but my breasts under the dress were bare, and my nipples peeked through the fabric. The soft brush of the cloth and the feel of Syl at my back had them peaked. My sword hung from the light sheath at my back, and I knew the effect was a stunning contrast to my darker skin and amber eyes.

My tattoos showed perfectly through the dress, their silver and white curls contrasting beautifully with the gown's transparent white. There was no hint of scarring from my beating yesterday. Goddess, had it been only yesterday?

A murmur rippled through the waiting warriors. Syl towered over me from behind, and I felt his heat radiate through me. Kharis turned my way, narrowing her eyes when she took us in. A flash of disbelief crossed her face when she scanned my unmarred skin, but she schooled it immediately into a blank mask.

"Kharis," I said, my voice strong enough to carry over the crowd. "I do apologize for my tardiness, but I was…distracted this morning."

Random chuckles went through the crowd that silenced at the Queen's dark glance. "Distractions can be dangerous, Teagan," she said, turning her ice-cold gaze to mine. One eyebrow arched even as her eyelids lowered, and I felt the chill in her gaze from paces away.

"They can also be enticing," I responded, turning slightly to run my hand down the side of Syl's face and letting it trail down the etched muscle of his chest to tangle in the ring on his nipple. He kept his posture perfect, and his eyes lowered.

I hated this. Hated treating him like an animal I could pet whenever I chose. We had talked about it before leaving, and I knew we had a role to play, but that didn't mean I had to like it. He was a person: a man, not a thing. They had assured me it was okay and that they took no offense, but how much of that was nature and how much nurture? Could a being raised as a slave understand the casual cruelty such actions implied?

I didn't think so, but there was naught to be done for it. "It is, after all, the week of our joining. I should have time to play with them, yet here I am, dressed and out of bed already. Such a disappointment." I snapped my fingers, and as one, the men knelt at my feet, perfectly balanced on one knee, their heads up but eyes pinned to the floor.

Startled gasps sounded from a few around the room, and I quirked one corner of my mouth up in a slow smile.

"Stay put, loves," I said, running my hands softly over each one of their heads. I gazed at them fondly; there was no lie in that look. I was fond of them. They did not respond, not even a twitch. Their behavior, for once in their lives, was perfect, though mine was not.

"I would like to send them to work early, Kharis. I find that as much as I enjoy their talented lips and gentle ministrations, I need a bit more time to myself to accomplish things like showering without a cock in me," I said, my eyes meeting hers in calm defiance.

Warriors around me laughed out loud at that and no doubt wondered what I had done to make my Trio so compliant when they were infamous for being otherwise. Kar had told me how he never felt an actual desire to please a woman, and I also insinuated that they couldn't keep their hands off me.

"I've never been fucked so often in my life, and I could use a bit of a break so I can begin to walk right again," I said, idly running my hands through Kar's black locks and smiling down at his head. He sighed under my touch, and Kharis's eyes snapped to him.

Around us, other warriors noticed the intimacy I shared with them. That was my goal today. I placed a kiss on Kar's head as an afterthought. I wanted to kiss his mouth but knew Kharis would not tolerate an overt violation of the laws.

"Of course, Teagan," she said, her ice-blue eyes so narrow I couldn't believe she could see out of them. Her face was perfectly flat, but anger seethed from her, touching me like the hard edge of a knife. "They can go back as soon as the celebration is over. In fact, you can send them to the pens any time you tire of them," she added.

"Oh, I don't think I'll tire of them, per se, I just need a few hours a day to repair the deep, deep injuries they cause in their eagerness to please. I'll be right as rain upon their return to my rooms each night," I said with a conspiratorial wink at her.

She knew their bodies. I knew that. Even her brother had not been off-limits; I knew that too. There were no boundaries to her torture. She might know them better than I did, but what they gave me, they gave freely, and that was worth much more than the things she knew that I didn't.

"As you wish, Teagan, are you ready to move into your own house?" She asked, surprising me.

There were advantages and disadvantages to that I needed to consider.

"Not, yet," I've grown accustomed to my quarters, but soon we will take you up on your generous offer to give us our own place. I thank you," I inclined my head at her, conceding that show of respect, hoping it would mollify her. She raised her chin and left me in a swish of leather and steel.

I went to the tables of food and stacked a plate high, then went to lean against a pillar near my Trio to eat. As all warriors do, I used my fingers and indelicately shoved bite after bite into my mouth.

Around the room, warriors and their men began to move again, casting looks my way. When I was full, I refilled my plate and walked over to the men.

I fed them with my fingers, and they ate. Slaves were allowed to eat at these events, but only after his warrior had, so I broke no law there. Where I did break the law was by feeding them. After each bite they took, I ran my fingers softly over the curve of their cheeks in a gesture of caring. This had been Kar's idea. He is a strategist if ever there was one. I saw the furtive looks of other slaves and warriors and knew my behavior was noted.

"You're a tropical bird in a frozen land, aren't you?" I turned from feeding my Trio and met the eyes of the gorgeous woman standing behind me.

"I suppose I am." I reached between us, offering her my forearm in the traditional style of greeting. "I am Teagan," I finished.

"I know who you are," she said, gripping my forearm in return. "Kharis worries you will usurp her," the woman said.

She was tall, Fae tall, but she had curves where Fae had few. Long green hair fell in soft curls to her waist, and light blue scales covered her arms and neck, but not her face. Impossibly large eyes of the purest blue I had ever seen looked at me with faint amusement. She was breathtaking.

Four men stood with her, two at each side. They towered over both of us but were of equal height to my Trio, should they be standing. They dressed in flowing colorful togas, and their expressions mirrored hers.

"My mates," she said.

"Pleased to meet you," I said, reaching my forearm to each of theirs.

With wide smiles showcasing perfect teeth, they accepted my greeting. "I do believe the pleasure is ours, Teagan of Talamh na Sithe," the man on the right of the visitor said, and I knew they were not slaves just by those words. His soft voice resonated like a low, resounding gong, and those around us turned to look at the male who dared use his voice.

I wondered what they were doing here.

"I am Galene," she said. "Queen of Tir fo Thuinn," she finished as the spark of amusement grew in her eyes.

The men around her looked like fighters, but their faces were kind as they watched me. They were lovely, scaled in the same manner she was. Their ears curved like a Fae's, and their scales went higher on their faces. Long queues of shockingly blue, purple, aquamarine, and pink ran down their backs while purple eyes, yellow eyes, blue eyes, and green took my measure in one gaze.

"Well met," I answered, laughing heartily as my eyes swept the room. She belonged here even less than I, and we all knew it. Tir fo Thuinn was a realm layered under those above it, including Talamh na Sithe. It was a world nearly covered in rough seas. The people there were said to be fierce, and it was also said they were shapeshifters of a seagoing variety. They were thought to be peaceful and loving. They were not a warrior race.

Rumors that strong, strange magicks flew wildly there abounded. They were cousins of another kind; all of us from the same origins. That they had magic told me they were Tuatha de Danann, even though they had no ties to Talamh na Sithe.

"Circumstances make strange bedfellows," she said, looking over my shoulder at my Trio.

"So they do," I answered, turning to see Syl'ta's eyes were raised and locked onto the Thuinnian Queen. Fierceness he did not try to disguise radiated from every pore of his body, and the Sea Queen did laugh then, causing his eyes to drop quickly.

"Goddess, Teagan, but you get more interesting by the moment," she said. "I must go. I have already stayed in your light too long. It was a pleasure to make your acquaintance, and I hope that our future dealings are fruitful," She winked at me, her eyebrow raised, and the corner of her mouth turned up in challenge. The men bowed their heads in unison and walked away with Galene as they mingled through the crowd.

Pameline walked up as the Sea Queen left, "Teagan, you look amazing," she said, her wide eyes taking in my unmarred skin.

I lifted my shoulder in a shrug like it shouldn't be surprising that I healed so well. "Our Goddess's magic is strong, Pameline."

"I see that. I," she started. "I want to believe." She watched the crowd around us with an uneasy eye.

Here and there, glances flit our way, and more than a few were wary.

"Then believe. Faith is not a blind thing; you have seen the evidence. That is all you need to believe I speak the truth," I said, keeping a watchful eye on those around me.

Sighing, she said, "I am with you. Though it may mean my death, I am with you." She walked off, her men trailing after her.

I bid my Trio to rise, and together we eased through the crowd. They kept their eyes lowered as many a warrior in the room would look for an excuse to use their behavior against me.

On the other hand, I placed a hand on their chests here and gripped their fingers there. You might think these are small things, but in a land where one can't use pronouns when addressing her mates, it is not. These tender touches implied that I saw them differently, and I did.

I would have touched them more in any other land, but fire lasted longer if started from a spark and not lit with kerosene. As I mingled with those not throwing daggers with their eyes, I noticed more and more of them touching their own men kindly. I spoke with as many as I could, and each time I was asked about my wounds from the day before, I answered that I asked my Goddess to heal me, and she did.

I answered as though it were an everyday occurrence for a Goddess to heal them of mortal wounds. I kept it simple and did not preach. I left them to wonder and open their minds to the idea. The men would do more in the pens than I could in a room full of wary women.

Kharis found her way to the throne not long after I completed my first circuit around the room. She cleared her throat and glanced out at the sea of warriors, commanding their attention with her silence.

"We come together with the People of Tir fo Thuinn to seek an alliance. War has torn us apart, but I hope to find togetherness in peace," she started. "For generations, our people have been at odds, but our lands are too rich not to share the bounty between us." She paused, looking out at her people and watching their faces. "We were once One People, and we should be again. We can spread the ideals that make Eregion great to the lands beyond. We can be a great influence in the lives of those around us," she continued.

Looking around the room, I saw warriors shift and cast nervous glances at one another. Seems that not everyone was comfortable with the words Kharis spoke.

Though Eregion seemed peaceful, too many men and women had been stolen from their homelands to want the Eregion principles to spread. As far as I knew, this was the only land that operated under the premise that the most populous and strongest group of its citizens were kept as slaves. And though there was peace here, it was unlikely to continue, even without my intervention. A house built on sand and lies will fall.

"Free trade with Tir fo Thuinn benefits all. We've long held to the belief that our low birth rate is due to the limits of our genetic pool. With Thuinnian blood in our warrior ranks and our slave pens, this could change," Kharis said, and I felt my face flush with anger. I hoped Galene did not agree to this; I really did. I thought we shared a spark of commonality and would hate to find we did not. She could be a useful ally going forward.

The thought of men with pastel skin and hair in all colors of the rainbow forced into Eruhini slave pens made me sad. Away from their seas and in this unforgiving land, they would die, surely these two Queens knew that.

As Kharis spoke, Galene watched me, never taking her eyes off my face, and I struggled to keep my emotions from showing. Around me, I felt my Trio shift, and I fought harder to maintain a blank face so as not to draw attention to us.

"In return for fresh blood, coral, fish, and Thuinnian marble, we will fight any invaders Tir fo Thuinn may have. We will send engineers to build power grids. We will also supply valuable ores needed to complete the process. We will take

Thuinnian oil to convert to the fuels necessary to run our economy and show them how to do the same for their own."

I watched Galene's smooth face darken. Her expression did not change, but a shadow crossed her smooth features, and I wondered how much of this supposed alliance was voluntary. She quirked an eyebrow at me in challenge.

"An alliance between Queen Galene and myself will move both of our kingdoms forward, diversifying and expanding our economies. I will send my best social planners to her to implement the changes we have found fruitful in Eregion. We've enjoyed almost two thousand years of peace since we moved from harsh, unproductive patriarchy into a warrior class matriarchy."

"The males in her lands are free, she hasn't faced problems with them yet, but they will come. Together we can quash any ideas they might have to give themselves a larger voice. We don't need their voices. Other parts, yes, but not their voices," she said, looking around the room with a warm, wide smile as chuckles broke out among the warriors below.

"Part of our agreement is that she will allow us to form similar policies there that have been so successful here. Long Live Queen Galene and Long thrive Tir fo Thuinn!" she shouted. Shouts of 'Long Live!' echoed through the vast hall.

Whistles and the pounding of glaives sounded for many minutes until Galene came to the dais and waited patiently for them to silence.

"I thank you for the warm welcome, Warriors of Eregion," she started. Her voice rang like a bell over the heads of those below her, and it caught my attention. "We come today to begin a relationship with Eregion that I hope will continue long past my reign. The Eregion people are bold, beautiful, and loyal to their crown, like the Thuinnians. I pray to our Goddess that she finds this alliance pleasing and blesses us with a long relationship." She paused to look over the silent denizens, seeing no reaction, her brows furrowed.

I wondered if she knew this was a faithless land, a land without magic, a Goddess, or a soul. Kharis straightened her spine at the mention of The Goddess, watching the Thuinnian Queen more closely. I caught Galene's eye and gave a faint shake of my head.

"An alliance between Tir fo Thuinn and Eregion will benefit us both, and we look forward to seeing the fruits of it. We will begin to transport females of the highest quality for warrior training and our most desirable men to your trainers in three months.

"Your engineers will return with us to build the necessary docks and transport stations on the wild and unpredictable shores of our realm before the transport of our people can begin."

"In the meantime, we brought with us loads of oil, food, and coral as a show of good faith." She smiled at the women below her, and I felt something else in her words. Magic.

Her voice wove through the crowd, binding those around her. To what end, I did not know, but I felt the magic in my tattoos and my soul as surely as I felt my heartbeat. I arched an eyebrow at her, watching her intently. Her magic did not feel offensive; if anything, it felt like the soft hand of love caressed those it touched.

She was planting another seed, and I felt it take root.

"It is my honor to enter this alliance with the people of Eregion. Enjoy the gifts we brought and in three short months," she said, staring pointedly at me, "You will enjoy the unique gifts Thuinnian men have to offer. At that time, we will begin the process of engineering our society to mirror yours," she finished. She inclined her head to the crowd below and moved from the dais as her mates followed.

She continued to roam the room, her mates trailing after her. They shook hands and accepted congratulations from warriors and slaves alike. I watched as Galene's mates tried to engage Eruhini slaves in conversation and were blocked by their warriors in most cases, but not all.

Three months. I sighed. That was her challenge to me. She did not wish to send her men to Eregion as slaves; she did not want Kharis to change her society to reflect ours. I felt the sweet softness of her magic and knew she did not want to harden her lands with the icy touch of Eregion. She might not want an alliance at all.

A land of peaceful sea people would be no match for a force of Eruhini Warriors. Perhaps it was a case of alignment or fight, and she chose what she hoped was the lesser of the two evils, I did not know, but my supposition felt right to the core.

As she spoke, she made her pact with the Eregion people, not Queen Kharis. I wondered if Kharis noticed the slight change in verbiage. If she had, she did not correct it. She might think she would rule this land forever, but her days just got markedly shortened to three months or less.

The Goddess wouldn't allow full-grown Thuinnian men to come here to die at the whims of this cold, unfeeling land, and neither would I.

It was one thing to be born into this society but another to be thrown into it. Some might survive, but most would not. The other stolen that came before me and I, myself, are proof of that. It was coming anyway; it just needed to happen faster.

I gripped the fingers of the men beside me and squeezed them. I felt Kar's warm strength at my back as Syl and Lyros squeezed back. I hoped they understood what had just transpired.

We mingled a bit more, talking to warriors who might be receptive to change. Pameline did the same; I watched as she worked the room. She had been here longer, knew more warriors, and would have a better feel for our position among them.

I touched my men, a caress here and a glance there. We weren't obvious enough to arouse anger, though we did get many curious looks, and that's what we wanted. I walked with sovereign grace through the crowd, keeping an aura of magic around me. I wanted them to feel my power.

The more questions we raised, the better. Now that we had a timetable, we needed to step up our efforts to make people question what was going on around them. Not only that, but she also wanted them to question their Queen.

After another pass through the Hall, I went to our rooms to change. The men were expected at work, and I had training with Pameline in advance of a mission scheduled for the week after.

They waited while I changed into leather training pants and a matching sleeveless shirt, allowing my tattoos on my arm to show. Though the lands around were frozen, the palace was kept warm by the magic of electricity and the age-old method of burning wood and their precious black ore.

We had not talked about the Queen's statements, either of them. A sense of heaviness followed us as we moved through the palace on our way to start a revolution.

They followed behind me, not because that's where they belonged but because heavy thoughts distracted them. It's one thing to talk revolution in the safety of our rooms and another to breathe oxygen on the spark of fire like a bellows.

It was my duty as my Trio's owner to drop them off and pick them up from their ascribed duties. Regretting each stop more, I first left Kar in the smithy where ten other men already shoveled wood and black ore into the massive furnace. The heat was unbearable, and I wondered how they tolerated it.

Warriors and a few trusted men pounded metals into weapons. I touched his face, pleading him with my eyes to be safe as I left him, drawing stares from the other men and curious glances from the women.

Next, I walked Lyros to the stables as Syl'ta ghosted behind us with watchful eyes. The stables were one floor above the slave pens and furnace rooms. Suffocating heat radiated off of the stones in waves. I felt terrible for the men and beasts alike.

Horses snorted at the sight of him, and I laughed when he rolled his eyes. It made sense that they hated him, a wolf in the prey's den. At least now, he knew the reason for their displeasure. Over his shoulder, I watched men shovel stalls clean and pile in new bedding.

Hundreds of horses stalled on this level, and half that many men worked to make them comfortable, their backs marked with wounds old and new. Sweat glistened off them, but they made no notice of it.

The animals enjoyed more comfort than most of these men ever had, and the thought broke my heart. As I gripped his fingers tightly, I offered a smile. This was why we would fight to change this place. Win or lose, this land would change. Should we fail, another would pick up the mantle and fight on as the seeds of change were being sown. Once grown, there was no way to cut them down.

I watched him walk away, his scars glistening in the sweat that beaded on his back, and my heart grew heavier. They had not asked for this, and I had not given them a choice.

"Syl," I said when we were alone in the halls of the palace again. "You don't have to follow me. If you want, I can let you go. It may be safer than being by my side when the swords start swinging." I gripped his arm, stopping him, my eyes boring into his. "I'm no better than them; I haven't even asked what you wanted."

He crushed me against the wall, his hot tongue parting my lips and forcefully twining with mine. He kissed me hard, hands clamped onto either side of my face, so all I could do was allow it. I went limp, caged between him and the cold stone wall.

"Never offer that again, Teagan. We've made our choice. We chose you before you placed your hand on my spine and felt the first sparks of magic linking us together. I believe that. Your Goddess chose us for you, and with you, we will stand. I believe this too. Together we win, and together we lose. There is no afterward if we fail; we understand this," he said, following his words with another crushing kiss, and I felt him rise and part the leather of his war skirt.

"I need to feel you inside of me," I said, running my hand down the planes of his chest. "I need to feel something more than fear," I said, my voice shaking.

He pulled my shoulders around and pushed my face into the stone wall, ripping my leather pants to my knees in one, practiced swipe. Gripping my hips, he bent me over and pushed into me quickly, his bar hitting my cervix and slipping into the space behind it. I cried out, unable to stop myself.

I needed this. During the celebration with two Queens, fear and doubt had planted themselves in my mind. Fear of the future and doubt about dragging anyone into this fight with me. I did not doubt that the cause was just; I doubted that I could win and feared that I would take three lives needlessly into hell with me. The pressure was too much, and I lost sight of the fact that I had the backing of a Goddess. The Goddess.

With each snap of Syl's hips, I achieved clarity. Pressure built in my womb, and Syl ripped an orgasm out of me with his skill. I braced against the wall and on my forearms and cried out again as his strokes lengthened and came harder. The slap of flesh echoed through the halls, and I didn't care if one hundred warriors witnessed this beating I took.

He jerked me up to him, wrapping his forearm around my throat to restrain me while thrumming his fingers over the core of me. I came apart, shattering the fear and doubt, replacing it with something more substantial and fitting of a warrior woman.

Releasing my throat, he pushed me over into the wall. I caught myself on my hands as he pounded into me with enough force to lift my feet from the ground. A final thrust, and he came with a shout, burying deep inside of me as he spent himself. He trailed his hands down my spine, his head thrown back while he struggled to catch his breath. He pulled away, and hot, thick semen ran down my thighs.

I rested my heated face against the cool stones while the pounding in my chest fought to ease. Slow, loud clapping pulled me from the peace drifting over me, and I straightened.

"Interesting, Teagan. Very interesting." Ang'ali moved from the bend in the passageway that served to conceal her. She was with another woman whose face I knew but whose name I did not. "On your knees, slave," Ang'ali demanded, snapping her fingers at Syl'ta.

He did not immediately fall to his knees. Instead, he met her eyes, quirked a smile, and fixed the panels of his skirt to cover himself before slowing dropping down, using me as a brace.

I straightened, taking the time to stretch my back like a pleased cat before pulling my pants slowly over the swell of my hips. Her face reddened with anger at my show of satiation. "I thought it was interesting as well, Ang," I purred, shortening her name, knowing she hated it.

"I'll see you whipped again for the laws you broke, Teagan. Allowing him to come in you, how base," she sneered. "And to let him take you in that manner, very unbecoming of a warrior, Teagan, to allow him to have a position of power over you." Her cold laughter echoed through the stone passage.

"Ang," I whispered, so she had to listen to hear. "I begged him to come in me, to fill me with all the amazing seed he has. Maybe he'll give me a baby. I hope so. And that position, Goddess, that piercing hits all the spots. I'll have them all take me like that tonight; I mean, they reach so deeply inside of you and the pleasure? Amazing. That you limit yourself is sad. If you ask me, maybe a good fuck against the wall would get that oversized stick out of your ass.

"I broke no laws. Everything Syl'ta does to me, I beg him for, plead for. Not my fault that when you had them, you squandered the opportunity to discover all the pleasures they have to offer." I curled my lip and scanned her square body in disgust. "Up Syl'ta," I said, "We have work to do."

My black-haired king rose to my side, his blue eyes flashing, and Ang'ali drew her sword, barring my way with it. I had my sword at her throat before she could draw her next breath. "If you draw your weapon against me again, it'll be the last action you take." My sharp blade drew a thin line of blood across her neck, and she stepped back, allowing us to pass.

Turning my back on her, I walked away, holding Syl's fingers in mine as I went. I could feel her eyes boring into my back as we went, and I didn't care. Not even a little bit.

Ang'ali was one warrior I would never win to my side and to show her anything, but brute strength would invite trouble. She was a bully, and the worst thing you can do with a bully is back down.

She went through Trio's like cordwood, and most of them did not survive her. She will talk. Word will spread. And none of that mattered because what one warrior heard, another would hear differently.

One warrior might hear that I held Syl's hand or that he brought me such incredible pleasure my knees shook. Another might hear that he touched me reverently and not out of fear. Those are the women I wanted this quick mating in the hallway to affect, not that we planned it that way. It could work in our favor.

I did not miss the high blush and soft 'O' on the warrior's face next to Ang. Her story would be different, and I hope she told it well.

I left Syl at the Boucherie and made my way to the training gym, where Pameline waited with the sweet smell of spice and heather that marked me as Syl's mate trailing behind me.

Chapter Fourteen

Syl'ta

I went into the storeroom to wash up and grab an apron; my hands shook as I reached for it. I clamped them together to stop the tremors. It didn't help, and they wormed their way through my body until I sank against the wall, a trembling, shaking mess. I fought to control the spasms that shook my body and failed.

I knew Teagan was a warrior, most Erhu women are, but she is not Eruhini. She is filled with so much light and heat that it is easy to forget she has a fighter's soul. After that moment, I would always remember that Teagan is a warrior.

Ang'ali is twice her size and a hundred times more brutal, but Teagan marked her throat with her sword that moved faster than the eye could track, daring Ang'ali to challenge her further. Ang'ali backed down, and I will remember that moment forever. The only reason Teagan is not First Sword is that the Queen does not fight newcomers. I've seen my sister fight; she is no match for Teagan in speed or strength. I saw that now.

Ang'ali has twice the mass Teagan does, and it matters not. Teagan's power choked the air from the tunnel and danced down her sword. She is fierce. She will be Queen; I saw it as plainly as I see that her eyes are golden, and her skin is brown. She will be Queen. She gives not one fuck about the rest of it.

I sat in the dark as my racing heart calmed. I wasn't expected today. The butcher was a kind, old woman with knowing eyes and a decent heart. Stolen long ago from a softer place, she never made warrior rank, but her skill with meat kept her in the capital.

"Trouble, Syl'ta?" she asked, using my name as only one other female does.

"No, Madame," I said with a sigh, fighting for composure. Ang'ali could make our lives miserable. A word from her could end not only Teagan but the rest of us as well before we had a chance to grow a revolution.

"A lie," she said. Whatever place Madame Zaya came from had magic. She could sense a lie and a truth the moment words left the speaker's mouth. "You have lady troubles. Is your new Mistress unkind?" she asked.

"No, my lady," I said, knowing I have already said too much.

"Not a lie. Your new Mistress is kind to you. I know not her face, but I hear her name. She comes to me in visions, and I know what she's about. You too, Syl'ta. I know your heart, and it is good. The risks are high, but the reward is greater. I believe," she said, turning a rheumy eye my way. "Spread your tales here; you are safe. I have faith," she said, giving me a sly wink.

She closed the door and left me. I took a stuttering breath and got up from the floor, fastening my apron around my leather studded skirt. Opening the door, I picked up a knife and went to carve into the side of horned Cervidae before me. Zaya referenced faith and belief in much the same way I had with Teagan and my brothers. Maybe she did see, and perhaps she spoke the truth.

"Hold your knife this way, boy, and thrust up into the vital organs of the thing here, and here," she said, taking the knife from me and expertly sliding it between the ribs of the beast. "The heart is at the fourth rib space and the lungs the fifth. For the heart, you must slide under and toward the middle, and for the lungs, you must slide straight in. Both can be reached from the back as well." Deftly, she put my hand over the knife and guided my hand in quick thrusts through firm flesh.

"The liver is on the right, tucked squarely under the ribcage. Stab through any of the lower ribs or up through the diaphragm," she said, guiding my hand upward through the meat of the thing. "Any of those strikes are fatal, Syl'ta. Remember that.

"Your mistress's heart is pure, and should this knife disappear and be sewn into one of the panels on your skirt, I

160

will not miss it." She turned and walked to the front of the store where other slaves worked piling cut meat into the display case.

I stabbed into the carcass over and over, experimenting with the force needed to cut through flesh and bone. Surely Eruhini bodies with beating hearts were softer than the dead flesh of an animal, but possibly not. I used as much force as necessary and then some so that it felt natural. Then I delicately cut the ruined meat away and sliced the rest into steaks, chops, and the other cuts warrior women loved. The leftovers I ground into what we slaves ate daily, for we did eat well. A starved slave cannot meet the expectations of their warriors.

I packaged the meat and placed it onto the cart for the others to unload. Oddly, I was the only one trusted with a knife. My grasp of the rules was stellar; it was the follow-through that got me every time. But Zaya had different ideas, and Kharis had long ago given up on taming the old woman. As her skills were valuable, she was left mostly alone.

"I heard your new mistress follows The Goddess and has magic," Zaya said during our afternoon break. She said it loudly enough to cause the other men to turn their heads.

"She does," I answered, turning to catch her eye.

"I hear she has great magic," she continued. "Healed herself from the lashes she took, so she did."

I laughed at the overt way she was pretending to have a casual conversation. The slaves here were used to her eccentricity and enjoyed it, or they didn't last in her service. "That's true, madame," I answered. "Not a mark on her."

"This Goddess must be powerful," she added, her voice rising.

I dipped my head between my shoulders and shook from laughter. "Aye, so it would seem. She says that any who believes can have magic and that we are all Children of The Goddess, men and women alike," I spoke to the floor, not missing the sharp intake of breath from those around me. "She also says that there is more magic here than her homeland of Talamh na Sithe, if only we follow the Goddess."

"We followed the Goddess in my homeland," Zaya started. "We had magic; I've just forgotten how to use it," she finished with a wink at me, and I knew she was lying. She used her magic in subtle ways, and no doubt, she used it all the time.

Throughout the day, customers came, and whispers passed over the counter along with packages of meat. High ranked house slaves and pets were allowed to shop unchaperoned. While I stayed in the back, carving meat and stabbing carcasses, the men up front spread fantastical tales about Teagan, magic, and Goddesses that I am sure grew with each telling.

By the end of the day, Teagan was riding dragons and making the moon rise. I heard snippets of their conversations and chuckled to myself, even as I worried about Ang'ali too. There would be retribution for Teagan's actions- and mine. Ang'ali bore watching.

My Trio's time with her was the worst in all our days, and I knew from personal experience that she would not let this go. She was by far the most brutal Warrior in the land, the Queen herself was not so cruel, and her cruelty is legendary.

Ang'ali had killed her last Trio as they did not please her. It was said she tortured them to death in secret chambers hidden below the slave pens. We had never been able to find those rooms, but I had no doubt they existed.

Her current Trio was so near death Kharis had pulled them from her and sent them to the pens' medical wing to recover.

Lyros, Kar, and I had spent nearly a year with her, and it was horrible. Her pleasure stems only from causing pain, and she is an expert at it. She would watch as others beat us or fucked us. She would engage in sex with us as well but preferred women and would often watch us fuck her lovers, then carve into our skin with her blade when we pleased them too well.

Kharis pulled us from her when it was clear we would be the next Trio to die at her hands, leaving Ang'ali none too happy. She would want revenge for Teagan having us, and she would want to make us pay for the show we unintentionally put on in the halls.

As the day wore on, I worried more. The sun neared the horizon, yet she did not come for me. It could mean anything and nothing, but my worry increased significantly as the shadows grew.

"She will come, Syl'ta. Eat dinner with me first; then, I'm sure she will be along," Zaya muttered as we worked to close the shop. I cleaned counters and put away tools, tucking a knife into the band of my skirt.

Lyros could sew as he often fixed the horses' tack. It would be nothing for him to make a pouch or three. I would pilfer knives as long as they continued not to be missed so that we would have them.

I ate a simple meal of stew with vegetables and freshly made bread covered in churned butter. I was silent as the shadows faded away into darkness. Still, Zaya sat, unconcerned, humming a tuneless song. Closing my eyes, I stilled against the wall and waited, praying for the first time to The Goddess, who calls herself mine, that Teagan was safe.

I waited until I could wait no more. As a man, I could not leave this place without an escort, or Teagan and I both would face severe punishment. But I was more than a man. I slipped deep behind my closed eyes and found my new magic. A painful shiver ran through me as I fell into the form of a large, white Artach Fox with blue eyes and a black streak down its pelt. After shaking my fur and eyeing the broad smile on Zaya's face, I slipped into the night.

Chapter Fifteen

Kar

There are no secrets in Eregion. None. I had been at work for only a few hours when rumors of Syl'ta and Teagan's run-in with Ang'ali and Rowana began to spread. Slaves are unnoticed here, and the walls have more eyes than warriors realize.

Where one slave gossiped that Syl was raping Teagan in the halls and Ang'ali interrupted, another whispered that Syl and Teagan were caught unawares in the throes of great passion and were attacked by the spiteful witch. I knew which rumor I believed.

The network of slave chatter is loud and extensive. Each slave stated that Teagan had pressed her sword against the larger woman's throat and drawn blood.

We would pay for that. All of us.

The thing the forgers liked most about me is that I rarely spoke, but once the rumors began to fly, that changed. I talked all day, quietly answering questions about Teagan's healing and magical powers. I waxed endlessly about her keen mind and kindness while not forgetting to mention her generosity in bed and liberal thoughts on sexual pleasure.

We are men, after all. We might be slaves. We might even be sex slaves, but we are still men who hoped for freedom and equality one day. If we could not have equality, we at least wanted a voice; we dreamed of a voice.

With Teagan as our ruler, we would have that. I felt it in my soul. I can't believe Kharis would bring a Fae to this place. Other races seemed more malleable to life here, but the Fae are notorious for their fire and independence. They are the antithesis of the Eruhini; Dark to Light and Fire to Ice. When our paths diverged, they grew even more so while we shrank, melting and twisting away under the mountains of snow and oppression that rule here. Or so it seemed from the outside.

Under Kharis's rule, we changed. We forgot. She killed her father so long ago no one remembers the King of Eregion. Oppression is insidious. It happens so slowly that by the time you realize what's happening, it's too late, you're on your knees, and the heel of the boot is above you.

It happens one step at a time, not in large waves. Each infringement is accepted until there is nothing left but rule by an iron fist in the end.

Should we win our freedom, it will never happen again. Once I pick up the sword, only death will part it from my hands. We will learn and move forward to make a better place. A place where fierce women can love fierce men, not enslave them.

I believed.

I kept the forges and the gossip running hot. I told no lies. I spoke of Teagan's thoughtfulness and her deep connection with her Goddess. I spoke of how the Goddess promised us power and freedom in return for following her.

Still, in this land, promises are like snow; they pile up and melt away on a whim of the weather. I knew not if my words carried any weight, but I knew they spread and built in the retelling.

And that was my goal.

At the beginning of my day, I was told to be silent a dozen times by the warrior swordsmiths, but by the end of the day, they strained to hear my words, not silence them. I worked harder than I ever had in their presence and let them think it was Teagan's influence in my life. The joy she brought made my hammer hit faster and shovel hold heavier loads. Maybe they believed she motivated me and wondered what influence that kind of esteem would have on their relationships.

I saw their speculative looks as I whispered to my peers while our watchers pretended not to hear. Other slaves and warriors came with their own tales no doubt spread from my brothers or created by others, and the fire built with such speed I knew that three months was no longer our timeline. If we survived three days in the heat of these flames, it would be a miracle.

As the day drew on and my muscles tired, I pulled energy from the ores around me to supplement my strength. I urged the coals to burn hotter and the metal to shape faster, and blade after blade was created in a way that had never happened before. The warriors supervising us began to whisper about magic, and I hid my smile.

Sweat poured down my back and arms as I made my hammer sing. The more magic I funneled from the earth around me, the more charged the air became. The forge smelled of Ozone and the violent thunderstorms spring brings. No one knew from where the magic came, but their eyes cut my way anyhow. I kept my head down and my lips loose.

My tattoos tingled with unspent magic, and I knew every word The Goddess spoke was the truth. The more I accepted it, the more my tattoos tingled. I wondered how Teagan managed to walk around like nothing was different or how she harnessed so much magic in her tiny frame.

Magic permeated the air and spread to the halls beyond. Those around did not understand what it was, but they sensed something was different. Eventually, I went silent again. My job done, to speak anymore would draw unwanted attention.

The afternoon wore on, and Teagan did not come for me. I knew she had training with Pameline, but it had not been her plan to stay long. There were no missions scheduled that we knew of, and we planned to regroup and train privately in the tunnels buried deep below the mountains and away from watching eyes.

I wanted to go to the pens and stay as long as necessary to evaluate gossip while gathering those supportive to the cause of freedom. I would talk of the Goddess and show my power to allies and encourage them to believe. Together, we could lay claim to the future and our destiny.

Afternoon turned into evening, and my unease grew. The warriors cast irritated glances at the door and wondered aloud where Teagan was. They wanted dinner and their beds and did not attempt to hide it.

I went to my knees and cast my eyes downward, saying, "Mistress, you may take me to the pens, and I will await my Warrior there," to the nearest warrior.

Sighing, she dropped her hammer. "Fine, pet, I will take you. I want a bath and my Trio; else, I would wait longer. You've been a model slave today. I will make sure Kharis knows of your obedience. Your new Warrior has done an excellent job taking you in hand." She petted my head idly, and I hated that she touched me at all.

I didn't think she meant to offend. She doubtfully figured I could be offended, but I was. Rising, I followed her broad back through the halls toward the pens, wishing for the comfort of Teagan and our bed.

Chapter Sixteen

Lyros

I hate horses, and horses hate me. Always have. Always will. They eyed me over their stalls, snorting and striking if I came too near. It was bad before but so much worse now that the wolf within was freed.

Usually, a kind word would calm the beasts, but there was no calming them now. The big fuckers knew a wolf walked among them despite my appearance.

I had no need to seek my peers out for gossip as they found me. A steady stream of men sought me out, asking questions, and telling tales. I was careful. Should I become suddenly agreeable, they would question my motives. Instead, I grunted and glared my answers to their questions, swearing and talking conspiracies as was my norm.

I trusted no one, and everyone knew it.

I spoke of Teagan in curious tones but wondered aloud about this Goddess of hers. Magic was dangerous, I said. Magic would lead to more oppression, not less. Yes, this Goddess had appeared to me and invited me to believe, but what were her motives? I chuckled inwardly as the eyes of the men I toiled next to took to heart the suggestion that magic was theirs for the taking, despite my warnings against it.

A person under the thumb of another will look for any way to level the battlefield. It was easy to spread the tale of magic and freedom while maintaining my guise of disbelief. In fact, it worked better than if I sang the praises of the thing.

More than once, I spit out that Teagan cared about our comfort and pleasure only to follow it with a statement about how little I trusted it. I mean, seriously? A female catering to my needs as a man? That couldn't be right. I'd watch their eyes go soft and distant at the thought of it as they walked away from me, shaking their heads.

When word came back that Syl'ta and Teagan were caught fucking violently in the halls, my work was done for the day. They said he held her by the throat and pounded away at her with feral abandon and that her cries of pleasure were so loud she disturbed the Queen in her sleep. I chuckled at the thought.

Males are still men. When I let it slip that she had placed her mouth on my cock despite my protests to stop, the men around me were converts, and I heard them praying to the Goddess that their warriors might slip up and do the same.

A prayer is a prayer, and I wondered how many slaves would feel that particular pleasure tonight as their prayers were answered. I mean, surely their prayers would be answered, right? If The Goddess wanted her people to believe in her, then

I figured she'd answer any request that came her way. At least for now. I chuckled aloud at the thought.

I used magic as I cleaned. The fresh ozone smell of it broiled from me, and my natural scent that Teagan describes as wild things and lightning deepened, sending the horses into a frenzy. I worked harder and faster than I ever had, cleaning stalls and replacing their bedding.

I had others help me move horses since I could not get my hands on them without risking death. I shook my head at their curious glances and suggested that maybe this weird Goddess made them afraid of me. Any phrase I said was repeated over and over, growing as it spread.

The stables were barely supervised, and Warriors came in and out only to have horses tacked and untacked. A few lingered, listening to the gossip that was common among the slaves. I saw their speculative glances and hoped this attempt to stir the pot did not lead to our death.

It was difficult for me to trust. I trusted my brothers, but just barely. We were all in the same poisonous pit, and I had faith that was a good enough reason alone for them to be trustworthy. I trusted Teagan somehow. And somehow, I believed in this Goddess, but it was not easy or natural for me.

I did as we planned the night before and spread what word I could, hoping I would not meet death at the end of the Queen's sword or worse as my words spread.

Shadows licked through the stables, and Teagan did not come for me. My reluctance turned to fear when the aisles darkened, and electric lights came on, and still, she did not come.

Most of the men had been picked up by their warriors, and only a few remained. Those few were assigned to stay overnight to see to the needs of warriors wanting horses or the horses themselves.

I slid onto a bale of hay by the entrance to the stables and waited. The air chilled despite the heat from the fires below and bumps raised on my arms. My tattoos tingled, and arcs of lightning shot from hand to hand if I placed them close together.

Something was very wrong. The plan had never been to remain at our duties all day. In this land where trust extended to the tips of your fingers and no further, I knew something was afoot. Closing my eyes, I went into a state of meditation, looking for my wolf. He ran as though he were being chased and ripped out of me, causing excruciating pain. My bones ripped from my body and remade themselves into sinew and fur, and I blacked out.

When I awoke, chest heaving and heart racing, the stables were in chaos. Pain racked my body as I dragged myself up and tottered out the door.

Chapter Seventeen

Teagan

Training with Pameline went well. As First Anvil, she wielded a war hammer with extreme precision and skill. The war hammer is a weapon I have struggled to learn. By its nature, it lends itself to extremely close combat, and the brutality of it is beyond anything I experienced with a sword.

The concept of it evaded me. Why engage in close combat when you can defeat your enemies from feet away using a finely honed length of steel? After she explained that swords aren't always practical and require more reach and space, I understood.

She demonstrated various moves on dummies made of cloth and the carcasses of inedible animals. I mirrored her movements and soaked up her insight into the weapon's weight and balance in my hands.

By mid-afternoon, my muscles were screaming, but the hammer sang in my hand like a finely tuned instrument. Pameline deemed me competent where before, apparently, I was not.

My sword had always been an extension of my arm, and only Airmed was better with one. According to the Captain of the

Swordsmen and her mate, Lann, she was better than he. Ari and I were a close match, and I knew I could best almost any enemy with sharpened steel.

Now that I understood the war hammer, I felt the same way. I flowed, striking quickly and moving through the training course Pameline had set up for me. It's impossible to spar with a hammer, but we did practice with our hands, simulating movements and strikes as if we fought to the death. I was First Fist and excellent in hand to hand combat, so I was hard to beat once I understood the hammer.

The training rooms were not private, and warriors came and went throughout the day, many stopping to watch our session. Word would reach Kharis, I was sure, but she expected us to train daily, and I couldn't help that I learned fast with an excellent teacher.

I had stripped my clothes down to the barest swath of fabric. My tattoos swirled on my skin as I danced with Pameline, bare feet tapping a staccato rhythm against the dirt and dust kicking up around us. I imagined the picture we made.

I didn't use magic to augment my speed or strikes, but I felt it there for the calling. Should I choose, I could be First Anvil. I knew that. Pulling Pameline into a hug, I thanked her. Even though she used a lash like a fiend, she was my sister here. I stayed longer than I planned.

Afternoon sun drifted through high windows, giving the illusion of warmth. I went to the showers to clean the sweat and dirt off, leaving Pameline to train her next warrior, and I wondered why I was not tasked with teaching swordsmanship.

Deep in thought, I heard the door to the shower room open and close quietly, but I did not hear footsteps. Feeling the charge in the air, I left my shower on and tiptoed naked into the changing rooms. Slipping the swath of fabric around me quietly, I moved again to the weapons room to pick up my sword and the hammer Pameline had given me. I slid both into the sheath I eased soundlessly onto my back.

"Where is that bitch," Ang'ali whispered. "She's in here somewhere; find her." Bodies eased through the empty changing space headed toward the sound of running water.

Pushing magic into my steps, I glided closer to the only exit in the room, hoping to get a better idea of the odds against me.

Four women, including Ang'ali, searched the room in silence, their graceful movements showing their readiness to fight. Carrying swords, hammers, and maces, they toed past other doors in silence, heading toward my abandoned shower.

"We'll get her first; then we go after her Trio. This ends tonight," Ang'ali said, and I stilled at her words.

If she attacked me and I killed her in self-defense, there would be no punishment, but should she attack my Trio, and they lift a finger to save themselves, they would forfeit their lives.

"Her clothes are here," another voice whispered back so softly that had I been in the shower, I wouldn't have heard it.

Their backs rounded the corner, and I heard the shower drape rip down. Using the clatter as cover, I sprinted out the door and down the halls leading to my men.

Footsteps behind me did not slow my pace.

"Teagan!" Pameline cried out as I raced through the training gym to the halls beyond.

Pouring magic into my legs, I raced down the halls, unsure where to go first. There were four of them and one of me. Should they split up, they could take the men I didn't reach first.

We had not planned for this. We had not prepared for so many things. Had we a contingency plan, I would have known where to go first. I reached out with my magic, searching for them. Maybe I could warn them somehow. They needed to run, and I had no way to tell them. It was my fault. I left them unprotected. Bile rose in my throat at the thought of Ang'ali and her friends getting to my Trio.

The Goddess said I could do anything with my magic, yet I had not taken the time to learn my limits before I shook the hornet's nest. Feet pounded harder behind me, and I knew they were hot on my tail.

"Stop her!" Ang bellowed, and I felt metal collide with my legs, tripping me.

As I fell, I saw the scythe skitter by. Blood ran down the wound it caused. I jumped to my feet, ignoring the pain, and backed against the wall so they could not encircle me.

"Four Ang? You can't beat me in a fair fight, so you bring friends? Don't think it will ensure your victory," I said, bringing my sword up.

"I'm tired of you, Teagan. You flaunt yourself and think no one will challenge you. I will challenge you," Ang'ali answered, her sword tip up and ready.

"You're tired of me? Yet you bring others to help you do your dirty work?" I tsked at her, watching her face go red. "You should be embarrassed. Four on one? That's not a challenge. That's an assassination," I said, shaking my head at her.

The women around her cast their eyes in Ang'ali's direction.

"It's not honorable, that's all I'm saying. Seems like behavior unbecoming of a Warrior to me," I taunted, wanting her to strike first. "It kind of makes me think you are a coward," I finished.

Before the last syllable of the word was out, she lunged. I grinned and felt the smile light my face. The other warriors stepped back, and I knew I looked insane. Wild curls flew around my face, and my teeth bared with pleasure from wading into the fight.

The sounds of swords clashing echoed down the stone halls.

"Engage her!" Ang'ali shouted when the others hung back.

"Leave now, and I will let you live," I growled, never taking my eyes off the giant woman in front of me. "Don't be the coward she is," I said, countering each clumsy strike Ang'ali made. "Not you, Ang. You're right; this ends tonight," I yawned against my free hand, and she screamed her fury at me, putting more force into her swings.

Ang'ali might outweigh me by double. She might have more muscle mass and strength, but she had little skill with a sword. Should she have picked the war hammer, I may have struggled, but she chose my weapon to use against me, and it was a fight she would not win.

Her friends saw that, and one of them dropped her mace and ran. The other two jumped in, and it became a new game. I quirked an eyebrow as they engaged me, and the smile that had formed on Ang'ali's face fell.

"You're a crazy bitch," she laughed or tried to. It came out as a wheeze. "You can't win. It's three against one; lay down your sword, and I'll take you to the Queen," she said, sweat already dripping from her prehistoric brow.

"No, you won't," I said, keeping all three at bay with my sword. If I'd had the one from Talamh na Sithe, it would be glowing now. I believed in this fight. I knew I would win. "Besides, I've done nothing wrong, other than making better use of the men none of you could handle. You should hear the sounds they make when they come. Goddess, they are delectable," I chuckled, slicing through the arm of the Warrior holding the hammer. It went limp at her side as tendons and ligaments separated from bone.

She had been trying to get to my flank, and I wanted to end that distraction. Her deafening howls drowned out the sound of steel on steel. Before the eye could catch the movement, my sword clashed with Ang'ali's again.

"You have no honor, Ang'ali. Are you challenging me for Second Sword? Yes, let's pretend you are so that there is a modicum of legitimacy to this fight. Now you," I said, addressing the other woman. "I have no excuse for you. Stay down when you lose your sword, and I'll let you keep your head," I said, stripping her sword from her in one deft move, wiping the cocky look off of her face.

She went for the sword at my feet, and I slashed across her shoulder, causing her to scream. "The next one takes it off. Walk away, and maybe you will live to be dishonorable another day." She raised her hands in surrender and backed away.

I caught a flash of white fur racing down the hall, and it distracted me, allowing Ang'ali to draw blood. I lost my sword. Enraged that she had managed to disarm me, I somersaulted into her, sweeping her legs and riding her to the ground while I took it up again with a loud battle cry.

I brought it to her throat as she attempted to buck me off with her hips. "You can't kill me, Teagan. If you kill me, the Queen will come after you with everything she has," she said, believing it. A sneer spread her face as she tilted her chin in defiance. I stood, twirled once to get the angle right, and took her head.

The warrior backing away from me turned and ran. I leaned against the stones, catching my breath. I hadn't fought three on one since I was a teenager, and Ari and the others ganged up on me after I stole her favorite knife and hid it under Arlie's bed. It was all in fun then. Not so much now.

I needed to train harder.

I lifted my head to see the white fox with startlingly blue eyes frozen in mid-step, staring at me.

"Sorry, I got delayed," I said, straightening up. "It's best you go to the pens until I clear this up with Kharis," I finished with a soft kick to the head at my feet. Find the others and let them know."

He whined softly, watching me with keen eyes.

"I know. I do. This came at a bad time, but there's nothing to be done for it. Find your brothers and go. I need to know that you are safe. Sneak in if you can, so they think you've been there. Don't make me order you. I might get out of this, but you would not. Please," I added at his pained expression.

He glanced at the body on the floor, turned, and slipped soundlessly away.

Grabbing hair, I picked up Ang'ali's head, squared my shoulders, and walked toward the center of the palace.

Chapter Eighteen

Syl'ta

As a fox, I ran. Fear is a great motivator. From shadow to shadow, I sprinted, praying I would be unseen. I rounded the corner and smacked into a large, silver wolf.

He growled at me, and I bit his ear, shaking my head. Using my smaller body, I rammed into him, turning him from his headlong run toward Teagan. He growled, and I yipped back, urging him to follow me instead.

My urgency must have gotten through his thick skull because he changed directions. Together we eased through the darkness, down the stairs, and into the backside of the pens. Using a high wall for cover, I thought about my man form. A shiver ran through me, and I was grateful to rise on two feet, not four.

Lyros stood beside me, his mouth open in question. Raising a finger to my lips, I shook my head, making a gesture to encourage him to stay low. I peered around the wall, surprised to see Kar leaning against the stones on the opposite side. His head was tilted back, face lined with worry. His eyes were closed.

Using columns and stones for cover, we picked our way to him. Settling on either side and adjusting ourselves, so it looked like we'd been there awhile.

"Any word," Kar whispered, not opening his eyes.

"Teagan got attacked in the halls by Ang'ali and three others. Ang'ali is dead, and the others ran. She fought like a force of nature. I've never seen anything like it. After, she simply picked up Ang'ali's head and stormed toward the main hall with death in her eyes," I said, my words ending in a sob.

I reached for my brother's hand. "She said she would come for us and that she could get out of this more easily if we were nowhere near. They're going to kill her. I feel it." Silent tears fell from my eyes.

Never had I seen anything like Teagan and that sword. She fought in the way that lightning strikes-here, there, and everywhere.

She was a storm, brilliant and deadly in her fury. The smell of iron, wildflowers, and magic was so strong that it boiled my blood. Because in her perfect violence, she was also beautiful, covered in the blood of her enemies. If only he had gotten there sooner, maybe the fight could have been avoided.

He felt his brothers stiffen. "It was terrible. It was beautiful. Goddess help her; they will kill her for this." I said, a silent sob wracking my body.

Kar patted my thigh, bringing his dark gaze to bear on me. "No, they won't. If Teagan was jumped in the halls, then the fight was dishonorable. Even Kharis can't punish her for that," he said, his voice calm and certain.

"It will be her word against theirs," Lyros whispered. "Syl'ta is right. Ang'ali is Kharis's pet. She will be furious."

"She can be furious all she wants to; Teagan did no wrong. Kharis's own laws will support Teagan," said Kar, his eyes glancing off a warrior headed their way. He silenced us with a nod.

"Your new mistress tired of you already." One of the pen's guards wondered by, kicking Kar's foot. He looked up, saying nothing.

"I mean, she's been rutting and moaning in the halls with all of you, yet here you are. Alone. For hours." The woman's gray eyes met his as she scanned his face for a reaction.

"Cat got your tongue," she laughed. "Teagan must be a hell of a warrior to tame you," she glanced at me, and I lowered my eyes, biting back a retort.

A month ago, I would have mouthed off to her, earning myself or my mistress the lash, but now I lowered my eyes in model submission.

"Never thought I'd see the day; she must be magic after all," mumbling, she walked away, scanning the line of men waiting in the pens as she went.

"I don't like this," I said.

"Neither do I," Lyros echoed.

Kar leaned his head back, closing his eyes again. "I have faith," he said.

Around us, the pens settled. Unbound slaves stayed in the lowest level of the giant palace near the furnaces' endless heat. Some waited to be chosen as a warrior's Trio, though that was rare as few females in the land didn't already have one. Others waited for assignments to various jobs or to perform services that earned their keep.

There were far more males than females, and many men died in the pens without ever being chosen unless there was something about them that drew a warrior's eye. A few warriors went through slaves like laundry, killing with impunity for their pleasure. Ang'ali was one of those people.

The only reason we survived her was that my sister pulled us before it could happen.

Other groupings seemed happy. Many warriors kept their Trios forever, never forsaking them. I sometimes caught their soft smiles and kind words. Those warriors were not unlike Teagan, I suspected, and saw their men as something more than slaves.

My Trio had been fought over, passed around to please this warrior or that.

Kharis used us for political currency, and we had spent little time in the pens.

As the warrior receded from view, a Trio of men scooted over to us.

"Is it true what they say?" One of the men said, casting a worried glance at the warrior guards.

"Which thing?" I said, keeping my voice low.

"That your Mistress is magic and that you have magic now too." He scooted closer so he did not have to strain to hear my words.

"It's true," Kar answered for me. "The magic comes from the Goddess of her People. We are their cousins, light to dark." He opened one eye, pinning the other man with a glare.

"If we are their cousins, why does this Goddess not give us magic?" he asked, lowering his voice.

"Do you believe you have a Goddess?" Lyros countered.

"No," the other man answered immediately.

"There you have it," said Kar, resting his back and closing his eye again.

Though we planned to spend time in the pens, spreading the word about Teagan and her magic, worry frayed our minds, and as we said nothing else, the other man moved away. We had said enough, anyway.

Servants laid out a meager meal of bread, dried meat, and water, and we filled our bellies, trying to calm our nerves.

Afterward, with nothing left to do, we settled against the wall and waited to hear what fate befell us.

Chapter Nineteen

Teagan

"I was attacked, without challenge by her," I said, pointing out one of my attackers. "Her, her, and her," I pointed at my other two attackers and shook Ang'ali's head in angry defiance. "I challenge the three survivors to an *honorable* fight. Three on one are acceptable odds." I chucked the head to the side, raising my sword as I waited for the three warriors to respond.

The room stilled, and Kharis turned from a food-laden table with odd slowness. Her eyes widened when she saw my gruesome souvenir, turning the full weight of her angry gaze on me.

My bold entrance was a gamble. By calling the three other women out publicly, I was hoping to avoid a situation where they banded together and made up another story. I stood, sword at the ready, waiting for their response.

"We didn't know she planned to attack you!" the first coward said, backing away from me.

"You were carrying a mace, a hammer, and a sword, respectively. You tripped me with a scythe. How could you not know?" I growled a low warning, letting my blood-stained biceps flex, my body naked, but for the single swath of cloth I escaped with.

The other women had cleaned up and hidden their wounds. I wanted mine to show.

"Fight me now, in the way of a Warrior, and not as a coward," I challenged.

"Is this true?" Kharis said, turning her dark glare on the three women in question.

"I can explain, my Queen," one of the women stepped forward, and I leveled my sword at her throat.

"Did Teagan attack you?" Kharis asked, her eyes cold and voice so low the clamoring women around us silenced to hear her.

"No," the first woman to run said. "She offered us an honorable way out. Ang'ali stalked her in the showers and attacked her in the passage as she went to pick up her Trio." Her eyes widened with fear, and I saw how young she was. If she were twenty, It would come as a surprise.

"And you ran at the first clash of swords, Ro'ya," the woman whose arm I slashed rounded on the younger girl, curling her fists. "Had you stayed, the outcome would've been different," she sneered, slapping the girl in the face.

"The outcome would've been four dead warriors, not one. Anytime you want to fight me honorably, make the call," I yelled, my voice carrying across the marble floors to bounce off the sleek, stone walls. Roars sounded from the crowd, and bodies pushed our way.

"Enough!" Kharis boomed, her voice silencing the uproar from the warriors around us.

"These women attacked you alone, Teagan? Where is your Trio? They are no stranger to a fight," she asked, her face flat but her eyes calculating.

"I was delayed from picking them up, my Queen," I snarled, carefully aiming my anger at my remaining attackers. "I do not know where they are," I finished.

"They are in the pens, Kharis. I escorted one myself and saw the others there as well," an old woman stepped from the crowd, and I recognized her as the butcher. I also saw the twinkle of the lie in her eyes.

"And when did you escort him, Zaya?" Kharis asked, her wary gaze turning to the lady.

"The sun had not yet begun to set," she answered, and that was the end of that as the blood on my arms had not dried, nor my wounds healed.

Had the men been involved, their death would have been swift or slow, depending on Kharis's mood. But they would have died.

"I escorted the forge slave known as Thalakar," another woman said, stepping forward. "It was not yet late, and I believe, as well, that the others were already there," she finished, casting an approving glance my way.

"What do you say to this challenge, Warriors," Kharis turned her icy eyes on the three women.

"I have no challenge, your majesty," the young girl who was the first to run said with a deep bow. She would grow and learn from this.

"I accept that," I answered, nodding her way.

Relieved, she backed up to stand by an older warrior who smacked her on the back of her head.

"I have no challenge, my Queen," The next started, "She beat us fairly in an unfair fight. We did not act honorably, yet she did. I offer my apology." She bowed her head, waiting.

"I accept," I said through gritted teeth.

"She killed Ang'ali, and you're just standing here and ignoring your sister's head. Her literal head. Fight her, attack her, take her down!" the final woman screamed as she advanced on me.

"There is no honor in an ambush, Jordania. You were taught better. There is no challenge, for she already beat you. I strip you of your command and your Trio. You will receive five lashes for your crime. When you prove that you are the Warrior I raised you to be, we will discuss your future." She stopped the other woman's protest with a glance, her face filled with barely contained rage. "Anyone who wishes to fight

Teagan will challenge her in the way of a Warrior. Is that understood?" She finished, not waiting for an answer. "Come, Teagan, let us collect your men."

She swept by me, tightly controlled rage seeping from her pores, the temperature next to her colder than it should be. I moved in beside her, shivering from the chill. I said nothing as I followed her from the Warrior's Hall and into the stone passageways.

Deep inside the heart of the Palace, she stopped me.

Turning the full force of her anger on me, she said, "Go, Teagan. Leave this place. Take your Trio, if you want them, and go." Her eyes were as flat and frigid as I ever saw them. Piercing me with the ice-blue of her rage, she continued. "You've stirred up enough trouble with the talk of magic and Goddesses. Just go. Take a horse, your slaves, and leave." She was shaking as she spoke, whether it was rage or fear. I did not know.

"I can't go back. You, of all people, know that. I have done nothing wrong. You wanted strong warriors, and you got one. I've played by the rules, Kharis," I said, watching her face as the anger left.

"Ang'ali was like a child to me. I can never forgive you for this," her voice rang like chimes, and I believed her.

"She did not intend to let me live, and, had I died, I wouldn't have forgiven myself either. I didn't ask for the attack, Kharis.

There was no cause for it. I simply answered the call; it's all I could do." I inclined my head to her, watching her calm at my words.

She walked away, and I caught up to her. Neither of us said a word on the way to the pens. I worried about the men but knew they were safer there than with me. Could I take them and go? Maybe, but that was not our destiny.

I doubted Aramea would welcome me back, especially not with three silver men in tow. Our future lay here. This raw, desperate land had become my home, and I would do my best to see it freed.

Chapter Twenty

Kar

She walked through the pens with Kharis, swathed only in a thin, muslin wrap that did nothing to cover her nakedness. The blood did more to shield her body from the wandering eyes of the men around us because she was covered in it. Her sword was sheathed across her back and a bloodied hammer at her side.

She walked straight to us with ethereal grace that was both commanding and terrifying in its beauty. Kharis stood in her shadow, and everyone that saw knew who the Queen of this land should be. Magic rippled from her, causing gooseflesh to rise on the arms of the cowering slaves, and I knew her appearance would do more for the rumors than any words.

Teagan ran her hands over Syl'ta's cheek, then reached for Lyros, tenderly caressing his shoulder. She dropped a kiss to my uptilted face, and I felt Kharis bristle.

"I apologize, my Trio, I was delayed. I'm glad that you were delivered safely in my absence." She reached for my hand, pulling me up. "Let's go home."

Every face turned at her words, male and female alike.

"You are too free with them, Teagan. It goes against everything we believe. You need another Trio before you become too attached and make mistakes that will cost you," Kharis said, her voice dripping with icy disdain.

"They are mine. That is your covenant with your warriors, Kharis. As long as I want them, they are mine, and I want them." The smile she gave us made my dick instantly hard, and I shook my head, lowering my eyes before Kharis could see my reaction.

"Guard," Kharis yelled, and I froze, fear filling me and chasing the warmth of Teagan's smile away.

"My Queen," the guard nearest snapped to attention as Kharis strolled to her.

"When did Teagan's Trio arrive?" she asked, narrowing her eyes in our direction, and my fear grew deeper.

"The dark one got here first; I'd say mid-afternoon. The other two came later, but not much. Well before the evening meal," the guard answered, and I stilled, holding my breath. Other than going behind the wall to the latrines, they have been where they are all night.

I smiled inwardly. A woman seldom saw a slave as an individual, and we had been together as a Trio since maturity. The guards saw me and saw my brothers though they were not there.

"You're sure?" Kharis asked.

"Yes, Kharis. This Trio is in the pens so seldom that we noticed them immediately.

"Very well," Kharis sighed, and I could feel her tension mounting. "You are dismissed, Teagan. Take your Trio and consider my offer. I hope you change your mind and accept it.

Teagan inclined her head and asked us to rise. We dusted ourselves of the hay and dirt that covered the pen's floor. Moving in behind Teagan, we walked toward the gate. She said nothing and did not look back.

As we moved into the passageway, we heard the Queen pick a Trio of men to ease her wrath.

We said nothing as we walked the stairs to the passage that led to our rooms. Teagan didn't look at the body the cleaners were wrapping in cloth. Blood ran into the center of the stones and splashed up the walls around. Girls with soapy buckets scrubbed the rocks and did their best to remove the stain.

I recognized Ang'ali's body, even without her head attached to it, and my fear spiked anew. Teagan had killed her. I knew Syl wouldn't lie about that, but it was one thing to hear and another to see.

Teagan reached out and grabbed our hands, holding them tightly and pulling us up beside her. The girls stilled as they watched us walk away.

She opened the door to our rooms and crushed my mouth with hers before I could close the door. Her hot tongue found mine, and she moaned into me. She was shaking with the adrenaline a good fight leaves behind and sought to ease it. Pulling the others to her, she ran hands over their chests and arms, worry etched on her face.

"Are you alright?" she asked, breaking the kiss and shivering against us.

"Teagan, we're fine. You were right in sending me to the pens; you saved us." Syl pulled her in his arms, rocking her back and forth. "Everything is okay," he finished.

"Everything is not okay." She pulled away from him, crashing into the stone wall of Lyros.

He wrapped his arms around her, kissing her neck softly. She moaned against her will, arching her rear into him. "I'm bloody," she said, her breath coming too fast and eyes growing too round.

She scrubbed at the blood on her arms, trying to free herself from Lyros grip.

But freedom isn't what she needed. She isn't the first warrior to be horrified by their actions later, justified or not. Had Teagan walked through the door, grabbed a bite of food, and a shower, I would have thought less of her.

Even though it was necessary, her reaction to the violence proved she was the woman I thought she was. I closed the distance between us, stilling her arms where they tried to dig into her flesh.

"Shhhh, Teagan, let us care for you," I said. Her body trembled harder, threatening to come apart. I silenced her with a kiss. I felt one of my brothers relieve her of the coarse fabric that barely covered her.

Our hands were everywhere, forcing her to think about anything but what happened in the halls. We would talk later, but talk is not what she needed.

Unspent adrenaline has a way of lasting for days, making one jumpy and less focused. She couldn't afford that, and neither could we.

Picking her up, I took her to the bed, following her body down and immediately placing myself between her thighs, thrusting into her hard. She cried out, and I crushed her mouth, silencing her. She didn't need gentle, and I would not give it to her.

My brothers lapped at her nipples, the only part of her not covered in blood. But the blood of our enemies made her more desirable, not less. She was a true warrior. Filled with heat and passion, she killed for what she believed in, not for enjoyment.

I punished her with my hips so that she would not punish herself. I snapped into her, my strokes unforgiving. I could do this all night, and I would until she was relieved of any misplaced guilt and the adrenaline that poisoned her faded.

Syl pulled her hair, arching her neck so he could shove his cock into her mouth, and she fell apart. Shattering around me and gripping me so tight, I had to think of cleaning latrines to keep from filling her. She wasn't ready yet.

I rolled her, placing her on top of me, pinning her legs between mine, it tightened her already impossibly tight core, and I shuddered. Using every bit of my training as a slave, I held out. Syl pushed back into her mouth, and Lyros positioned himself behind her, slowly easing his cock in next to mine.

She arched and cried out. "No. I can't take it," she said, going limp between us.

"You can, Teagan. And you will," Syl said, gripping her hair tightly and pulling her face up to meet her eyes, his cock still stuffed in her mouth.

When she relaxed around us, we started to move, and the sensation was incredible. The feel of her walls and Lyros's cock against mine was so delicious; I knew I couldn't hold on much longer.

Lyros took over the work, pounding into her and moving us with his thrusts. A scream ripped out of her; Lyros latched onto her nipple and bit it gently. Her head dropped despite Syl's hold, and he let it. Taking in the sight of us tearing her apart. She came, clenching two cocks with enough force to slow Lyros, and I let go, filling her with my seed, my cries adding to hers.

Undeterred, Lyros picked up where I left off, pushing my spent cock from her body. He wrenched her from me, placing her between him and Syl'ta. Lyros pulled out with a sharp slap to her ass, and she arched again, whimpering at the feel of it. He slapped it again, bringing a beautiful red mark to the meat there.

Syl slid under her as Lyros pulled her to her knees. The looks on their faces fiercely tender. Using the wetness from between her legs, Lyros slid into her sweet ass. He moved slowly until fully seated while her howl tore the air. Syl silenced it by entering her again and slamming his mouth into hers, drawing a trickle of blood. He shoved into her, and her cries became whimpers, and she went limp between them.

They worked her. Maybe harder than she wanted, but it was what she needed. They broke her apart and rebuilt her without the chinks in the armor. The memory of sweet submission now replaced the ones created by betrayal. Letting someone else control the situation instead of always being the one in charge of the decisions would go much further than talking it out.

Maybe we needed it too. We'd taken women in every way possible, but never without their direction. Teagan might tell us we are men and that our opinions are valued, but this divine moment of her yielding completely to our wills healed more than words could.

Through it, we saw our worth. And hers.

That she trusted us to handle her roughly and give her what she needed spoke volumes. To her, we were worthy. Actions speak, in this and all instances, much louder than words.

The intense concentration on Kar's face as he pumped into her faltered. His eyes met mine, and I knew he felt the same thing.

Worthy.

We had never been deemed worthy of anything. Our sex had been demanded but not wanted. Our work in the Capital was necessary but not integral to its survival. Any slave could do those things. It's what we were trained to do. We had been replaceable our whole lives.

But this was something new, this feeling of worth. From the dirt floor and pain of the slave pens, this woman found us and deemed us *worthy*. A man's value is measured not in words but in actions. And those two things are very different. Only we could deliver Teagan from the doors of doubt.

She whimpered again as Syl thrust deep, his balls slapping on the meat of her ass, as he slapped his hand onto her round cheek again. Her breathing came harder, and she groaned, coming once more. He arched back and emptied into her with a shout. Only his arms held her up, and I was afraid she had passed out.

Lyros rammed into her twice more and stilled, his face going slack with pleasure. I smiled as Syl laid her down, our seed drenching her and spilling out onto the bed beneath.

"I'll run a bath," Lyros said, easing from her.

"Make it a hot one," I said, giving him a wink.

He grinned, shaking his head.

We had never been happier, and it showed on all our faces. This volcanic Fae had done more in a few days than a hundred or more women had done in a lifetime, and I loved her for it.

That's what this feeling in my gut had to be. Love. It went deeper, settling itself into my bones, and I felt the pain of it. I watched Teagan sleep, mouth softly open. So comfortable and free with us. So unguarded.

When the bath was ready, I carried her in and slipped into the water with her in my arms. My brothers and I washed her reverently, soaping her from head to toe. She sighed but did not awaken. Syl used the mixture on her hair, and we scrubbed until all traces of blood were gone. We rinsed her and ourselves.

Lyros put clean sheets on the bed, throwing the others in the corner. Arranging her between us and covering her with furs, we slept.

Chapter Twenty-One

Teagan

I awoke with a start. The feeling of the approaching storm dragged me from the deepest of sleep. My body was deliciously sore and tender in all the best places. Languid as a cat, I rolled to my feet, taking up the sword one of the men had placed by the bed.

Placing my fingers to my lips to silence them as they startled awake, I tiptoed to the door, engaging the lock with a soft snick.

I felt them coming toward us. With nowhere to go, I gestured toward the mirror. Lyros held up one finger, asking me to wait. On silent feet, he walked to one of the hanging tapestries, pushing it aside.

I felt my eyes round as he removed the bar from the door hidden behind the tapestry. My men keep secrets, I thought.

He eased the door open as I heard the sound of a key placed in the lock. We dove for the mirror, leaving tangled sheets in our wake.

"Search the room; they must be here," Kharis said, stepping in and raising the lights.

"It reeks of blood and sex. The Fae are base creatures, rutting like animals with animals." Hel'r stepped from behind Kharis, sword drawn.

The Queen's own sword dangled at her side. For all her talk about honorable fights, she came to assassinate us. She did mean for me to leave this place, one way or another.

We watched through the glass, knowing she could not see us. They split up and searched the room: the Queen, Hel'r, Evar, and Ronin, who made up her sometimes Trio. They all held swords and looked like they could use them.

"They aren't here, but look," the one called Evar pointed at the passageway. "They've gone this way."

"But why?" Hel'r asked, his eyes hot with rage. "They couldn't have known we were coming."

"No," Kharis said, "They couldn't have. They are up to something somewhere else."

"What now?" the other man said. Ronin was his name, or so I thought.

"We wait," Kharis answered. "This failure costs us nothing; she doesn't know I'm going to kill her by any means necessary. Let her spread her lies and tales of a false Goddess. When I hang all four of their heads on the palace gates, the others will forget. If they do not forget, I will kill them. This Goddess cannot help them now." With one final glance around the room and a lingering look at the mirror, they left.

"This Goddess can help you now." A chuckle sounded behind us, and we whirled as one. Kar pushed me behind him in a protective gesture, and The Goddess chuckled again. "You are doing so well, Teagan. Even better than I hoped. You should hear the prayers I am getting from the Eruhini. They've begun to find their magic." Her smile brightened her face, making it even more beautiful. "You can release her, Kar, but I applaud your protectiveness."

Slapping him fondly on the shoulder, I walked out from behind him. She wore a sheer lavender gown that made her eyes glow purple, long silver hair hung straight to her waist, and a thin circlet of silver crowned her head. In her hands were four swords. I recognized my blade from Talamh na Sithe.

Forgetting our nakedness, I reached for it. Smiling, she placed it in my hands. I ran my hands over the crafted steel. Tracing the runes I thought I would never see again in speechless wonder. It glowed faintly red as it picked up my aura.

"Thank you," I whispered, bowing before her.

"These blades were made for your mates by Ari's Laith. As you prepare for war here, so prepares Talamh na Sithe. Your victories are not independent of one another. To truly win, both lands must be free," Dani said, handing swords to the men. "Someday, Ari will call on you to help her defeat Aramea, and you and your people will go. She will not know to whom she is calling, but you will hear her battle cries. Between now and then, you must train slaves to be warriors and warriors to want freedom. Defeating Kharis will be the easy part; the rest will be hard fought." She stepped to me, taking a curl and tucking it behind my ear.

"Dani, I don't think we have enough. Not enough training, not enough allies, not enough time. You seem sure that we will win, but I am not so confident," I said, curling into her warm touch.

"You have more than you know, and you are far more than enough. Learn your magic and teach them theirs. Remember, there is very little that you cannot do. Only one has more magic than you, and she is yet to be born.

"Ari's daughter?" I asked breathlessly.

"Ari's daughter," she confirmed with another smile. "Perhaps, she will take my place someday, and I will retire to a white sandy beach to be waited on by handsome cabana boys.

"Your path is not to be a Goddess but to be a Queen. It's almost time, Teagan. Be strong and know that I will be with you every step." Bowing her head, she paused, then turned and walked away.

When we turned back, Kharis and her Trio had gone, leaving our room untouched. Had we not seen them enter, we would not have known they were there. We stepped back through our mirror, moving to bar the doors instead of just locking them.

"What now?" Lyros stood in front of me, arms crossed and face fierce.

"Now, we fight." My feral grin spread, and my teeth bared.

We moved the furniture aside, making a large area on which to practice. The men took up their swords, testing them for weight and balance.

"They are heavier than an Eruhini sword," Kar said, bringing the blade up and testing the straightness of it with his eye. If Laith made the sword, I knew it would be perfect. As somewhat of a sword maker himself, Kar would recognize that. "There's magic in it," he stated once finished with his inspection.

"Aye. The maker is the land's only Metalsmith that can imbue a blade with magic," I answered. Watching the way he looked at the blade.

He touched the runes etched into the multi-layered steel. The blade was so finely made it looked blue. The pommel was made of Stag antler and intricately carved with runes to add grip. Gold inlay made the runes shimmer, and I could feel the magic in the blade. It was different than mine, even though Laith had made that one too. Laith had been practicing.

"A man made this?" He brought his eyes to mine and caught them; the soft look of wonder made me sadder than anything I had seen in the awful place.

I took a deep breath. "Yes. Perhaps, when our lands are One, he will teach you. He is the last of his kind, and maybe your Goddess magic and his are the same." His eyes misted for a moment, then he grabbed me to him, kissing me fiercely.

"Thank you, Teagan," he said, pulling away.

He brought the sword tip up, placed a hand behind his back, and tried to parry me lightly.

"While you are strong enough to hold the sword one-handed, Kar. These Great Swords were made to be gripped two handed so that they slice through heavy armor," I said, reaching over and placing his hands on the right spots. "For thrusting, you can use it one-handed. Like this," I paused, showing him the proper position for both the thrust and the strike."

Together, they practiced holding, thrusting, and striking with their swords. They had acted as practice dummies with lighter swords before and had some knowledge. I gave them more.

We worked late into the night, I taught them as best I could, and they learned. More than once, their blades glowed, then stuttered out when they noticed. Lyros's blade glowed a silvery-blue, Kar's a molten red like my own, and Syl'ta's a surprising purple. My men had deep hearts and even deeper souls.

We practiced pulling magic and augmenting their movements with speed and accuracy, and I learned something new about Laith's work. The sword wanted to strike.

I had the skill to put my edge where I needed it, but magic made their swords cut true. I had no doubt a wound with those swords would be fatal. I wished I could get more for those who would fight with me, but those blades were priceless. That Laith made three for my untrained men was humbling.

With that being said, my sister was giving me a new blade when next I saw her. I chuckled to myself, imagining Ari with one of these fantastic swords. Someday, it will be an honor to fight back to back with her again.

When our arms grew heavy and our eyes tired, we stopped for the night. Not even bothering to shower the sweat off, we collapsed into a heap and slept.

Chapter Twenty-Two

Lyros

Teagan is a glorious creature. She showed us how to use our new blades with patient but exacting passion. Which is precisely the way she does everything. We are quick studies when allowed to learn. Before dawn, we had a modicum of understanding of fighting with a sword. We would get better in short order.

Piled together in the dead King's giant bed, we slept peacefully. I did not fear another attack by the Queen. She had made her opening salvo and thought she got away clean. She would be patient now.

As soon as we were up, I would start stealing swords from the armory and hiding them near the pens. Even without skill, the number of men there could cause some damage. If given the time and motivation to learn, perhaps they could win us a revolution.

She lay curled into my side, her breaths slow, and even and I could not believe the path that had opened before me since she came into my life. Soon we would be free. Or dead. Freedom sounded better, though, and I believed that we could win.

I watched as she slept and wondered how one with so much weight on her shoulders could be so light as if she had no cares. Her face twitched, and she smiled, causing me to wonder what she dreamed of.

"Is this normal?" Kar asked, shifting onto his elbow to peer at Teagan's face.

"A better question is, will she change? Once things settle, and she achieves her goals, will she change?" Syl'ta answered.

"I don't think so," Kar said, leaning over to tuck a curl behind her ear. "I think this is who she is. She doesn't waiver. These thoughts and convictions of hers are not new to her. A man made the magic swords The Goddess gave us. A Man. That is the place from where she came. That is her normal."

We watched her for a while longer, then began to rise. We showered and dressed, letting her sleep as long as possible, but as the sun reflected more forcefully off the snow outside, we went to wake her. She stretched and yawned, trying to pull the covers over her face begging for more time.

Finally, Syl stole her covers, and she came off the bed with a glare and a screech. We stood innocently, looking anywhere but at her naked body, shifting from foot to foot.

"Fine," she growled, stomping her cute little feet as she headed to the shower.

My brothers and I oiled our battle skirts to a dull shine, then polished the studs on the leather that crisscrossed our chests.

As a slave, we wore nothing else. The leather panels of the skirt overlapped and covered us completely. Even with quick movements, we did not expose ourselves. Still, they parted easily, giving warriors access if they wanted.

Teagan came from the bathing room, less irritable and beautifully put together. Most women wore their standard Warrior leathers daily. Teagan often chose to wear filmy dresses and occasionally soft pants. Today, she wore her black fighting leathers, which covered her from neck to ankle, with a cutout diamond at her bosom to her collarbones to allow for freedom of movement.

She had pulled her hair into a tight braid, and it laid flat against her head, making her look sleek and deadly. She had lined her eyes with kohl, something she never did. The addition electrified the black circle around her iris.

She looked otherworldly, stunning, and dangerous after strapping both swords to her back and a knife to each arm. To that, she added her war hammer, not bothering to clean the blood from it. After the events of yesterday, she was taking no chances.

With a wild grin, she beckoned us to follow. We walked on silent feet toward the breakfast hall, where voices rang out, and a scattering of laughter echoed toward us.

The Queen had once offered Teagan her own house yet had said nothing more about it since the turn of events. If we had our own home, we would have a kitchen, and one of us could have made meals there. Once a Warrior is gifted a home, one of her Trio must cease his other duties to care for it. Should it ever happen, I hoped it would be me.

That would solve my horse problem.

It would also solve this public dining hall issue.

When we walked into the hall, heads turned our way, but the conversations didn't cease. Kar, Syl, and I sank to our knees along the wall, clasping our hands and lowering our eyes. Teagan walked forward without a backward glance and picked up plates, loading them with food before bringing them to us as was required, only usually the women ate first.

She went back and filled her plate last, keeping an eye on us as she glided through the crowd, saying hello to those around her as she ate. Taking the temperature of the room along the way, she stopped and talked to those that engaged her.

And many did. I expected problems, but there were none. As she walked, warriors either stepped away or into her, griping her forearm and talking with animation. She had done something incredible and likely didn't realize it. Like her or not, Teagan had earned the respect of these warriors.

From her place on top of the dais, the Queen's glittering eyes followed Teagan's progression around the room, noting every handshake and whispered word. Being often ignored, slaves have the perfect vantage point to spot the signs of discord others may not see.

There was discord everywhere.

Teagan and her Goddess wanted a revolution, and they were going to get it. What that meant for us, I didn't know. She stopped, putting her head together with the Lashmaster, Pameline. How Teagan could be friends with the woman who almost ended her life spoke to the vastness of her heart. Their heads pressed together a long while, Pameline nodded once and walked away, chatting with others as she went.

The Queen stood, her eyes following Pameline. "Warriors, good morning," she started, interrupting Pameline's travels. "Today, some of you will embark on a mission to the Sléibhte Glasa to meet with clan Luchorpán to pick up a shipment of gold, cloth, and sword quality steel. You will deliver some of our finest finished swords, glass, raw iron ore, and the coveted black mountain ore they use for fuel but do not have naturally.

"Another faction will go to Tir fo Thuinn and meet with Galene to pick up another shipment per our agreement. Teagan, you will lead the warriors to the Luchorpán, and Jordania will travel to see the Thuinnians." The Queen's eyes swept the crowd, her face devoid of any emotion.

The leniency she granted Jordania in the light of day did not go unnoticed. Warriors looked from one to the other in confusion. At the same time, she was sending Teagan on a suicide mission. Luchorpáns are deadly folk, and only the most experienced negotiators go to them.

Yet Teagan gave a sly smile at the news, and I wondered what she knew that we did not.

"First and Third regiments of warriors will go with Jordania, and Second and Fourth regiments will go with Teagan. Mount up in half an hour." The Queen stood, walking away. Her Trio trailed behind, all of them smirking at my brothers and me over the crowd.

They did not intend for Teagan to return, and they meant for the Luchorpán King to end her so that Kharis didn't have to.

With a sinking feeling to my soul, I rose as she came for us. She shook her head once to silence my concerns. Only when we were alone in the stone halls did she speak.

"Don't worry. It will be fine," she said before we could get a word out.

"Teagan," I started. "The Luchorpán…" She crushed her lips to mine, silencing me. I melted against her heat, going limp.

"I know." She gave me a wink as she pulled away. "I've got this," she said. "I'll be gone for two days, at least, and maybe more. This buys us time. With four ranks of warriors away, only a skeleton crew will remain, including Pameline. Now's the time. Train your trusted men hard, so they are ready on my return." She took off at a brisk pace, and we followed behind, casting worried glances at one another.

"But what if," Kar started, begging her to pause just a moment.

She silenced him with a kiss, then moved to Syl'ta and did the same.

"No what-ifs, my loves. None at all." The smile that spread across her face was beautiful and confident. Yet, she refused to say anything more. "Do you want to go to the pens or to work?" she asked, hustling forward.

"The pens would be better so we can gather the men." Syl picked up his pace to match hers as she was practically skipping.

"Excellent idea, Syl. Come with me to the stables first," she said, a merry twinkle in her eye confusing me more than I have ever been confused in my life, and that says a lot.

Luchorpáns are notoriously nasty. They will kill you as soon as talk to you. I'm sure that is what Kharis intends, yet Teagan began to whistle a light tune as she skipped ahead of us. My brothers and I cast long looks at one another as we tried to decide if perhaps she had snapped. Maybe this land had finally gotten to her, and her mind was lost.

Syl shrugged his shoulders, and we three sped even faster to keep up with her loping gait. I saw Kar smirk and stretch his legs into an odd skip, and then we were all doing it. Laughing like loons, we slid to a stop in the stables, drawing the eye of the warriors waiting for their leader.

Chapter Twenty-Three

Teagan

I chuckled inwardly at my Trio's discomfort. I didn't do it to be rude; I simply didn't have time to explain. Yes, the Luchorpán are exceedingly dangerous, but I'd dealt with them before and had every confidence that things would be fine.

My concern was for my men. Even though there would be few warriors here, there would be some, including Kharis. I worried for their safety far more than I feared for mine. Besides, Pameline would stay behind and help them train those they deemed trustworthy.

When I got there, my horse was ready, and I pulled each man to me, kissing their mouths while the waiting warriors watched. I cared not one bit. Their lips were soft, and they tasted sweeter than any dessert I ever tasted.

Kar had carried my furs and draped them around my shoulders, raising the hood with a sigh. I turned to the only remaining stable guard, "Would you be so kind as to see that my Trio is returned safely to the pens. I'll be very agitated if there is so much as a mark on them when I return. I find their skin to be nothing short of perfection."

"Yes, Teagan," she said, snapping into a tight bow as if I were already Queen. Perhaps she thought I wouldn't return and did it as a show of respect; I didn't know which.

"Thank you, Aerolas," I replied, clasping her shoulder before stepping away. I mounted the white horse I usually rode, winked at my men, kicked the mare into a gallop, and ran out the door.

The wagons were waiting at the gates, and we circled them as their drivers urged the teams forward, and the ranks of warriors fell in line in front and behind the wagon train.

We headed South and East. The Luchorpán lived in the verdant mountains in that direction. The realms were not only side by side but layered above and below. Tir fo Thuinn was beneath us and was the largest by far, accessible only by water. Having never been on a boat, I would take the Luchorpán any day.

It felt good to be out; Goddess, it felt good. Being cooped up in the palace was stifling. Even in this frigid place, I would choose to be outside if given a choice. I just wished my men could ride beside me and enjoy it too. Well, except Lyros, he would have to run as a wolf, but I bet he would love that. I wondered how horses reacted to Syl'ta.

Riding my mare one-handed, I smiled, tilting my head to let the sun strike my skin. The breeze was cold but gentle, allowing the sun's rays to heat my skin. This place wasn't all bad. There is a beauty to its stark wildness that even Talamh na Sithe does not contain.

Snowbirds chirped in the distance, and a deep calm settled over our ranks.

"Mistress, you seem unfazed about going to the Luchorpán King." I glanced over to see a warrior called Tralalis riding next to me.

She was born Eruhini and showed it; sleek black hair framed pale skin and silver eyes. Her sharp cheekbones and pointed chin made her look cold, as most Eruhini do, but the merriment in her eyes spoke of more profound things. The tips of her ears poked through her shiny hair and full lips revealed even white teeth when she smiled.

"Luchorpáns are a fierce race, Tralalis; I look forward to meeting with them," I said, glancing over at her. She rode her white horse well, sitting naturally and comfortably as few do.

"They are deadly, Teagan. The last ranks of warriors that met with them did not return. Not a one." She did not look worried, and I liked her more for it.

"We will use our skills and walk away with fresh wagons in tow." I looked out across the snow-covered fields and watched as a snowhawk grappled with a white rabbit and flew away.

"And that's why I like you," she said, slanting her silver eyes my way. "You are fearless. I'm not sure there is another warrior that would have taken this assignment so willingly. You are different. It's refreshing."

"I thank you for that, but there's naught to be done for it. It's a dangerous mission, but one I am sure will be successful," I said, observing her expressions.

We rode at the front of the line, which in this direction is the most dangerous position. Behind us lay the Capitol, so the weaker warriors rode there. On the way home, we would reverse those positions.

It was a day's ride to reach the distant peaks and slow going because of the wagons, but the atmosphere was relaxed. We rode down the high plains and into the valleys below. As we traveled, the snow melted into dried grasses that blew in the warm breeze.

We stopped at the edge of one such meadow and let the horses graze while we ate a light lunch of dried meat and cheese. Some warriors had packed wine, and we passed the skins around, sharing it along with friendly conversation that somehow devolved into talking about men.

"Teagan, you seem rather fond of your Trio; I must say it's a shock to see them tamed," Tralalis said, stretching out to let the sun warm her body. Within minutes her cheeks were turning pink.

"Tame?" I threw my head back and laughed. "Only the weak-minded enjoy tame men. I appreciate their fire." I chuckled again, feeling the curls that slipped around my face catch in the breeze. "I've redirected their fire to other pursuits." I grinned at the thought of which pursuits I enjoyed most.

I caught the covert glances some of them exchanged. "Come on, ladies, surely you agree. All this eyes down and hold your tongue stuff is dreary. They offer much more than that," I finished, lounging back to let the sun hit my face too.

"In the quiet of my home, my men have freedom," Tralalis whispered.

"Mine, too," another warrior spoke up, and that was echoed by more down the line.

And then the conversation began in earnest. We talked about everything. It was just like being with my sisters; we spent far too much time lingering in the spring-like sun, talking about men's attributes- good and bad.

All the daring things my Trio thought I did, these women did too. They were women, and if any saw their men as slaves, they did not say. We laughed and talked about things that would scandalize Kharis. I knew these women would follow the path to freedom, and just like our conversation in the grass, if they disagreed with that, they would keep silent and stay out of it.

Too quickly, we mounted our horses and began the last leg of the journey. Slightly drunk and feeling light, we rode across the meadows, down another rocky mountainside, skirting boulders and deep gorges.

Hours later, as the sun sank low, we landed at the base of the mountain bordering on another meadow and into a valley below.

With good sightlines all around, I ordered the wagons stopped and camp made. I would take a few riders on to the meeting place.

Kharis had given excellent directions, but it wasn't hard to aim at the bright green mountain peaks far in the distance and ride. The road was well-traveled, and even the wagon passed with ease through most places.

"Tralalis and Vonali, you're with me, leave the wagons," I said, leaving the others to make camp and care for the animals. With any luck, we would be back and snug in our furs by full dark.

Saying nothing, we rode further. The air was warm here, and I had removed my cloak, leaving it at the camp. The evening sun kissed my skin with its marvelous light, and I felt my tattoos recharge. Kicking our horses into a gallop, we traveled the rest of the way alone.

A show of force would anger the fighters we rode to meet, and should this go sideways, maybe the other warriors could escape the fickle Luchorpán. In the distance, I saw the brilliant blue sparkle of a large pond, surrounded by a mist covered bog.

A rainbow curved through the fog into the sky above, and I knew we were in the right spot.

Slowing our horses, we walked to the edge of the wide clearing and waited. A war cry arose, and hooves thundered our way. Beneath us, our horses shifted. Tossing their heads, we fought to keep them from bolting in the face of whatever ran at us headlong through the bog.

"Hold," I demanded as the women beside me shifted. I crossed my arms over my mare's mane and leaned into her, relaxing my weight. Tralalis took in my casual pose, and her eyes widened. I winked at her.

The hooves approaching us thundered harder, and the ground shook. The horses shifted again, and the women wanted to turn and run; I could feel it.

"Hold!" I demanded, kicking one leg out of the stirrup and draping it over the mare's neck so I could jump off quickly. Vonali shook her head at me and fought with her mount to stand.

From the mists, riders came. Led by a man dressed in gold and green, they descended upon us. Fifty riders advanced on we three, and still, we stood. I stretched my back and stifled a yawn.

Dropping down from my horse, I handed Tralalis my reins and walked toward the approaching horde. They slid to a halt in front of me, and I continued to walk. I did not draw my sword.

As I approached the King, every rider pulled their blades. I stopped at his horse's shoulder, looking up through the veiled sun.

He smirked down at me and dropped from his mount, landing a full rod shorter than I.

"Teagan, my fair Fae consort you would be if Aramea were not such a toad," he said in the Fae tongue.

Smiling at him, I answered, "Wave your hands about and look terrifying. I have an army to impress," knowing the women behind me would not understand.

He took his arms and gesticulated wildly, causing the women behind me to take sharp breaths. "Lass, what are you doing with the likes of those cold-hearted bitches behind ye?"

"I was taken by Trolls and delivered to their Queen," I replied, raising my arms and answering his wildness. "Aramea planned the whole thing, so I could not go back."

"Ah, lass, make them pay for it," he chuckled dark and low, showing his black teeth with gold fillings.

"I intend to, Sir." He laughed out loud, tossing his head back. Wild red curls cascaded over his shoulder, and his soldiers put away their swords.

"Sit on my lap, lass, and learn what you're missing," he said, giving me a salty wink.

"That didn't work all those years ago in Talamh na Sithe, and it won't work now," I answered with my own laugh, and we turned and walked to where the women waited.

"You can't blame a King for trying. I wanted ye bad enough to offer Aramea wagons of gold. Such dark-skinned beauty would look lovely in my bed," he said, moving his arms and shouting wildly. I saw the warrior's eyes widen and marveled at the fact that they hadn't run.

"No blame at all, Sir, but you have four lovely wives that would have beaten me to a pulp," I screamed at him, placing my hand on his arm, and he patted it.

"True enough, that is, lass, true enough. They're pissing their pants, so they are," he chuckled as we approached my horse.

"Undoubtedly." I stopped at my horse, and he tossed me up onto her, his stature hiding the strength in his body.

"Lead the way then, lass. Let's see what ye have," he growled at the women, baring his teeth, laughing when they jerked back.

I turned my mare and kicked her into a gallop.

"What was that?" Tralalis demanded as she ran up beside me.

"Ah, well, he wants to see what we brought before he decides whether or not we live," I said matter of factly. I kept my face as somber as I could.

Kharis had sent me to die. Had I not known King Fendrel from his many visits to Talamh na Sithe, I may have. Despite their short height and adorable looks, they are vicious. They are also much stronger than they look and can rip a person in half should they choose.

Rumor of this interaction would spread like wildfire and could only help to increase my credibility. Let these warriors worry a bit longer about their safety; that was a small price to pay. Because of my prior relationship with Fendrel, they would leave this place with their lives.

We raced up the knoll to the base of the mountain where the women had made camp. As hoofbeats echoed off the stones around, they raised their glaives higher, holding the line.

Pride flowed through me. For the faults in the system, these women were brave. They would fight to the end, regardless.

"At ease, Warriors," I shuddered a breath, watching them.

Should they attack, this could still go wrong. I prayed to Dani that they would stay calm.

"The King will assess our goods. Stand down," I urged, opening a path for the King to our wagons.

"He brings no wagons, only the steel in his fighter's hands," a warrior stepped forward, blocking my way with her glaive.

"Stand down, Illon," I demanded. "Do not let your bravery turn into foolishness." I braced my mare against her weapon, and she dropped it, stepping back.

"This way, your Highness," I spoke to him in the Eruhini tongue so they would understand.

"Your wagons are light!" he shouted in the same language. "This is an insult. We bring our goods in faith, and Eregion sends nothing!"

Riding around the goods we brought, he scowled, and I worried, knowing that nothing was assumed here.

He switched to the Fae tongue, "She meant for you to die," he said, narrowing his eyes on me and gesticulating wildly.

"You are not wrong, Fendrel," I yelled at him, waving my arms.

"And what are your plans to redress this?" He stilled his mount, looking thoughtful.

"I will be Queen," I said. "I will use our Goddess's magic and defeat them. Danu has said as much herself. I lowered my voice, keeping it calm and steady.

He measured me for a long time. Silence stretched between us as his fighters and my warriors waited tensely.

"Then I will make a bargain with the new Queen of Eregion," he said. His smile spread across his face, taking some of the hard edges from it. "You will be my ally. Not Kharis. When you are Queen, we will align and right some of the wrongs done to these people.

"Should you fail, I will wage war on Eregion and tear it to dust and snow. Kharis works to grow her brand of society throughout the realms, and such poison cannot be allowed to spread."

"Agreed." I reined my horse one-handed and reached across the distance between us, gripping my forearm.

"A bargain is reached!" he shouted, his voice echoed across the mountains and into the valley below. He put magic behind it, and everyone around felt his words settle with a promise into their soul.

"I accept Teagan's word that future dealings with Eregion will be fair and more balanced. You will leave my realm with my goods and your lives," he said in the Eruhini tongue.

Heavy wagons appeared from the mists below and trundled our way, and I saw how meager our offerings were.

"And now we drink!" he cried in the face of my stunned warriors.

Jumping from his horse, he pulled me from mine and twirled me in a dance. His men dismounted, and a fiddle started playing while the women stood open-mouthed and staring.

I threw my head back, laughing as I danced with the King of Luchorpáns while his men lit fires and made camp next to my warriors.

I felt a little bad for the women. I knew how these men partied. Aramea always trotted The Eight out when they visited, thinking we made her more powerful, so we were witnesses to their ways. The visiting Luchorpáns left the courtesans exhausted, and the casks of alcohol empty.

Eventually, the women relaxed, put down their weapons, and joined in the revelry. The bonfires grew higher, and the voices louder. The warriors giggled and danced as the moon rose high over the valley below.

Tables sprang up, and we ate food reminiscent of the dishes from Talamh na Sithe, and for a moment, I felt like I was home. The food, the camaraderie, and the alcohol warmed my blood, chasing the Eregion ice from my veins. Goddess, it felt good.

The air stayed warm, and the enormous yellow moon seemed to settle directly across from us and join our celebration. I danced with the King and his men, drinking his sweet honey mead and enjoying the freedom of a summer night.

After hours of dancing, eating, sparring, and singing, the fires burned low. Fendrel and I moved farther from the sounds of fucking and the shrill cries of pleasure, choosing a spot where we could speak privately.

"How are ye setting about to win this fight, lass?" he asked, his voice hushed.

"My mates are teaching those they trust to fight. The women will have to choose, and I believe they want freedom. Who doesn't want the freedom to choose who they love and how they love them? That they fell into bed with your dominant males proves they aren't happy with the situation at home. The Goddess says we can win this fight, and I believe her."

"Your women are fucking my men because the Luchorpán fuck like Gods and have cocks disproportionate to their body size. I'm willing to fall on my sword and prove that, if need be, Teagan," he laughed, tossing his long flame-red curls from his shoulders.

Merriment and teasing shown from his green eyes, and I knew he'd no sooner fuck me than I would fuck him. His wives were gorgeous- and deadly. They'd have my head and his balls. He was simply a giant flirt.

I grinned at him, feeling it reach my eyes and make them twinkle. "Of that, I have no doubt, Great King. I am happy with my Trio of mates, even if not all the warriors behind us are. It's further proof of their dissatisfaction." I bumped my shoulder to his.

"Bah. Fine. No fucking," he grumbled, bumping me back. "If they think there was fucking, do not disavow them of the notion," he countered.

"Deal," I said, and another pact was born. Shaking my head and laughing, I sighed, feeling the mood grow somber. "It will be hard fought; I have no illusions. Kharis is strong, and her warriors loyal, but they have no magic. My Trio and I do. As more pray to the Goddess, they will gain magic also. I am hopeful."

"If The Great Goddess and Maker of All Things says you will be victorious, you will be victorious. I will call you Queen, and we shall dance in the Great Ice Castle in the north." He patted my hand, rising to leave me alone with my thoughts. "That will be a magnificent party; I look forward to it," he finished.

I watched as he went toward his tent, his short legs covering the ground in graceful strides. "As do I," I whispered. "As do I."

The moon was high in the sky when I left her warm rays and walked down the hill. Pulling my furs from the tent where warriors and Luchorpáns slept in piles, I laid under the colorful stars. Letting my body be one with the land below, I slept more peacefully than I had in ages.

Chapter Twenty-Four

Syl'ta

Teagan was right. Out from under the watchful eyes of their peers, the remaining warriors shuttered themselves away. It was like they knew a battle loomed and rested up for it. Pameline came to the pens, pretending to guard the men not sequestered with their warriors.

There was no man we did not train. Discontent was widespread, and none of them resisted. Could we trust them? There was no way to be sure, but my brothers and I talked endlessly of a future where we were free.

Should another warrior wander through the pens, we assumed our submissive positions. No man spoke up to tell of our treason, and I believed we were safe.

The clash of swords echoed through the halls, and still, no one investigated. No food was delivered, and Pameline herded a hundred men into the slave's dining hall where a paltry meal was laid. No man fought her.

She joked and laughed with us, eating dried meat on hard bread by our sides, and I knew what Teagan saw in her. We passed around flagons of water and soured wine unfit for a warrior.

Pameline was one of the few warriors that did not currently have a Trio, and other men watched her hopefully. From my experience under her control, I doubted she was much interested in men. She's always been kind, but she'd never been particularly interested in sex.

I thought perhaps other females were more to her liking but, of course, never asked.

Some men snuck off with other men in the pens and never showed an inclination toward females. When they were found out, they were killed so as not to spread the trait to their offspring. It was hard to imagine a land where, no matter what one's inclinations were, we would be free. With Teagan as our Queen, I believed the choice would be ours.

Would I change my mate? Goddess, no. And I prayed that Teagan would not either.

After our light lunch, we returned to the pens to train with old swords and other rusty weapons. Pameline taught the hammer and gave us every extra she had. We tucked them under the straw and hid them in the latrines.

Some of the men showed signs of acquiring magic, and we worked with that as well. My brothers were careful, not showing the depth of magic we had while still trying to help them. Nevertheless, we got better with it. Magic jumped to our fingers with a thought, and we found we could do many things with it.

The more magic one man displayed, the harder the others prayed. As evening moved into night and overworked muscles tired, Pameline stayed with us. Watching and working together, we discovered each man with magic had different gifts. They practiced with what they had, honing it.

Footsteps signaled the arrival of others, and we dropped to the straw, assuming the expected position. A meal was delivered that was even smaller than our lunch. Moving sluggishly as if weakened, we ate under the watchful eye of new guards.

Not wanting to draw interest in her presence, Pameline disappeared once other guards arrived. After the meal was finished, the new guards left, and Pameline did not return. Left alone, we rested.

The pens were silent; even the quiet whispering stopped. In the distance, a wolf howled, and a snow owl hooted. The stillness of the night was absolute. The furnaces heated the air to boiling, and I missed the softness of Teagan and our bed. I sat with my brothers, thinking that the day had been productive, when a shimmering light erupted from the middle of the pen.

Sleeping men bolted upright and watched as the shimmer turned solid, and a woman appeared.

The Great Goddess stood before us, resplendent in a sheer gown the color of moonlight and red roses. The men around us fell to their knees, trembling at the sight of her.

"None of that, friends, faces up, please. Do not cower before me; it's offputting." She walked through them, touching heads and shoulders as she went.

The stench of the pens was overwhelming, and she walked through it like a mountain meadow filled with flowers.

"You are mistreated, friends. Men as strong and as beautiful as you should be cherished, and I believe you will be. Not long ago, your people called upon me to help them, and I did. The false Queen has stripped my name from the history books and made you forget, but in your hearts, you remember. I am your Goddess, and you are my People."

"I created you from gold dust, sweet honey, and joy. You were made for sunshine and life, not misery and death. Follow me. Spread my name, and happiness will find you.

"Your true Queen awaits, and as tempted as you may be to turn all females asunder, do not fall into that trap for pain lies there. Nature is made of all things male and all things female. As a race, you must mirror that, and so you will."

"Your females have been hard, but that is all they know. Give them a chance. Together, you must build new roads to the way you are supposed to be, keeping what is good about life now and discarding what is not. Those are my words to you.

"In return for finding real balance, your magic will grow stronger and your land milder. The chill at the heart of this place is Kharis's heart. Magic and love will warm this land and make you prosper. Heed my words, children."

Every face riveted to her as she turned among the huddled slaves, taking in their faces. After a pause, she walked to where we stood against the wall.

"Dear friends, you have done well, as has Teagan," she said, pulling us into quick hugs that were not missed by the men around us. "I know you worry for her, but she will return to you unharmed, be ready. When she gets here, your war will start, for Kharis does not expect her to return and is celebrating the thought of her demise. She doesn't care that a hundred of her best warriors might have died with her; she just wants Teagan gone." She stopped, a slow smile spreading across her face. "Unfortunately, her celebrations are premature." She winked at us and was gone, her cloying scent lingering in the air long after.

Motion caught my eye, and I saw Pameline at the entrance to the pens, mouth agape. A look of shock on her face. Her eyes rolled back in her head, and she dropped like a sack of flour to the ground.

A group of men raced to check on her, and I knew that, as a people, we would be okay. They could have ignored her. They could have killed her where she lay, but instead, they placed their fingers on her throat and checked for her heartbeat. Looking relieved, they splashed water on her face until she came around.

Her eyes met mine across the crowd, and I knew she believed. She shook her head, and a broad smile that showed her dimples spread across her face. She eased to her feet, walking our way.

"Teagan will be back tomorrow then, later in the day. We have a few more hours. Rest now, I'll come at dawn, and we'll begin again. Shall I escort you to your rooms?" she asked, waiting for our answer.

"No, Mistress," I said from habit. "We'll stay with the others and rest while we can."

Nodding once, she said, "Call me Pameline, Syl'ta." Turning, she left us alone for the night.

Chapter Twenty-Five

Kar

We slept fitfully. As the sun came up, we were called to fill the furnaces and do the chores that are done daily. Silently we shoveled the black ore into the giant metal beasts that helped to keep the upper palace warm and the lower levels unbearable.

Once done, we returned to the pens to find a veritable feast waiting. Pameline stood with four other warriors, and they shooed the night turn guards away, shrugging when they commented on the size of the meal.

We descended upon the food, shoveling as much of it into our faces as we could. We were starved; the heat and hard work, making us ravenous. The warriors ate with us, and the smell of cooked eggs, warm meat, and soft bread layered over the stench of unwashed, sweaty men, making it bearable.

We trained more. With five warriors, it went better. They divided us into groups and worked with us. We had the muscle. We had the ability; they gave us the skill.

The men were given the weapons they used best, and the females spoke to us about tactics of warfare. They cautioned against simply killing every warrior we came across as hearts and minds can be changed. The bottom line being: women are still a rarity in Eregion despite the power structure. The loss of fifty warriors would be tough for future generations to overcome; the loss of one hundred might be unrecoverable.

Female children were so rarely born that the loss of one female life should be avoided. They urged us to use caution as no one wanted to anger the New Goddess promising us power and change.

As angry as many men were over their circumstances, they calmed with a detailed explanation of our situation. No female, except Teagan, had ever spoken to us in such a manner. They treated us like equals, and because of that, we did understand.

We fought and trained with them until sweat rolled down our bodies. They taught us warfare, but they also taught us social structure.

Again, no ranks of women came to check on us or wonder about the clash of metal coming from the palace's lowest reaches. We worked long into the afternoon.

Afterward, they walked us to the warm water pools so that if any came across us, we would not be breaking the rules.

The men bathed as the women spoke in quiet tones by the archway leading into the communal bath. Teagan had more followers than she knew.

We soaked days of dirt and sweat off our bodies and talked too. We had no idea what the day held. Not then. None of us thought that freedom would come easily. It might not come quickly, but the fact that we chose to do something, instead of sitting idly by straightened our spines and filled us with pride.

The looks on the other men's' faces were resolute. Did I want to die? No. Not when I had finally found a life worth living, but if my death meant freedom for my brothers, then so be it. That thought reflected on every face, Even the warriors studiously not watching us bathe.

We would live or die together. Be chained or freed together. The sense of unity permeated the air we breathed, and that is no small thing. Not in this place.

After our bath, the five warriors took us back to the pens, where we stretched out on fresh straw and rested while we could. No one could sleep.

Yellow stained light filtered through the windows, hinting at some strange storm to come, and I knew that storm's name. Like a summer thunderstorm, she would ride into the Capital. I am not a reader of the weather, but I know that hot and cold air clashes violently, often flattening crops and sometimes leveling buildings.

Teagan's flames burned hotter, and Kharis's cooled by the day. The two would meet, and lightning would strike. I could smell the ozone building and hear the soft sway of branches as the wind picked up.

We had done what she asked, and with the help of five women who now called us by our birthnames, we were ready. You can't fight a storm. You can move with it. You can survive it. But you cannot fight against it. Exotic things happen to physics when exposed to the absolute power of nature, and that is Teagan in a nutshell.

I'd been Eruhini my whole life and changed nothing. Teagan had been here half a turn of the wheel and would tear down everything and rebuild it into something better. I felt that to my core.

I lay on the straw, murmuring plans with my brothers, and waited for the sound of thunder to signal the arrival of our Queen. As the sun sank lower and the wind gusts came harder, I knew she was not far.

Chapter Twenty-Six

Teagan

I'm never drinking with the Luchorpán again. Mead is good but kicks like a horse the next day. Groaning, I rolled to my feet, stumbling after a skin of water. The sun had risen high over our camp, and the Luchorpáns were gone. They took the wagons we brought and left theirs without waking a soul.

Warriors stirred, groaned, and moaned around me, wrecked from a night with the cagey wee men. I wondered how many red-haired babes would be born ten months from now, for their people breed like rabbits. With a chuckle and a deep sigh, I relieved myself behind a bush then washed in the warm spring water that ran nearby. I rebraided my hair into a tight queue and pulled my furred hood to cover it.

I steeled my nerves.

As the women struggled to rise, I saddled horses and packed our camp. When they were able, warriors joined in, and we were ready to leave by midday, hours after I hoped to go.

The beginning of the trip was slow going. Women raced away to the bushes for one function or another; they would ride hard to catch back up to our wagon train; as the trip grew longer, their stomachs settled, and we moved faster.

Laden wagons did not maneuver as well as light ones, though, and there was only so much we could do about our speed. Tralalis rode in the back, and I kept watch on the sides, riding along both as we traveled.

Ahead a storm brewed, dark clouds gathered, and lightning struck cloud to cloud, but it did not rain or thunder. As the sun faded, the sky took on an eerie yellow cast that signaled trouble.

I was under no illusion as to what would happen when we rode through the Capital's gates. I just wish I had slept better. I pulled my white mare beside Tralalis and lowered my voice. "I'm going to kill Kharis," I said. "I'm letting you know because she never intended for any of us to return from this mission. Once she knows I live, there will be war," I paused, waiting to see if she would say anything before adding, "I'm telling all of the warriors that ride with us so that they can choose. I just wanted to let you know first."

She stopped her horse, her eyes pinned to mine. I pulled alongside. "You're going to what?" she asked.

"I'm going to kill the Queen." I met her silver eyes, unflinching.

She kicked her horse to follow the caravan, saying nothing for a long moment. "I respect what you're doing, Teagan, and I know it's the right thing. I do. You are a powerful warrior; let me think about it," she said, riding away from me, her back straight and her head watching the warriors she passed.

I hung in the back, guarding our flanks. Near mid-afternoon, I galloped to the front of the line and called for the caravan to stop. Warriors dismounted, stretched their backs, and loosened their girths. They stretched legs, spread furs, and sat to eat.

I moved restlessly through them, hoping my next gambit wouldn't lead to a fight. I stopped, standing beside their spread of blankets, and waited for them to look my way.

"Warriors," I started, taking a deep breath for fortification. "I stand before you as your friend and ally. You'd have to live under a rock not to know I disagree with some of the ways we practice as a people. I do not like that our men are slaves. They have value as so much more. Men are smart, funny, creative, giving, and kind if given a chance. Yes, they can be violent and hormone-addled, but so can we."

"I worship a powerful Goddess, and my People have magic. Your People and mine are cousins, yet you have no magic. I don't believe that's right. My Trio has developed magic." A sharp intake of breath went across the group. "They have also met our Goddess, for she is your Goddess too. Your people have been manipulated to forget her, and that's a mistake I would see remedied."

"Eregion is a great realm, and what makes it great are its people. You are loyal, brave, and proud. There is more strength here than in Talamh na Sithe, where most people have gone soft. You are hardy and persistent. There are no finer warriors. But there is more to life than being a warrior."

"If we don't have a choice, then life is forced upon us. Maybe you would be a glassmaker or a baker. Perhaps you love animals and would choose to train them. Life should offer a choice, and so should a leader."

"That we take infants from the bosoms of their mothers and treat their parents like livestock is unconscionable. That we force a man to breed a town and them kill him when he is successful is beyond anything I can tolerate."

"I believe in freedom, and I believe in fairness. I've made that no secret. I plan to challenge the Queen for First Sword, and if that means war, then so be it. I'm ready. I say this because I want you to have a choice in who you love, who you mate with, what job you do, and who you fight for."

"It would be an honor to have the support of the valiant Warriors of Eregion, but if not, then I will stay the course myself. This is not a call to arms. I'm not asking you to fight for me, not yet. I tell you my plans so that you can choose to stay out of the fight altogether. I have many allies at the capital, and they await my return. Should you not want to fight, you have the option of staying behind. We are near a village that I believe will shelter those who would rather wait and let the dust settle." I stopped talking and looked across the group of women frozen on the ground. No one spoke.

I was about to sit and eat myself when a hand raised tentatively in the air, seeking my attention. I looked at the warrior and nodded.

"You would allow us to return and fight the Queen against you?" she asked.

"Yes, I said. "That is, of course, your choice."

Another voice, "You would allow us to seek shelter and be safe in a village while the capital wars with itself?"

"Yes," I answered. "This fight is not yours unless you want it to be. I'm bringing the fight to Kharis because I do not believe her ideas should spread, and I want to see the people of Eregion choose their path." I stood, relaxed, hands clasped, and feet spread.

"If you win, won't you just take her place and institute your rule instead of hers," Tralalis asked from her place at the back of the crowd.

It was a smart question and one I'm glad she asked. "Yes and No," I answered. "I want to build a council that is representative of all the people in Eregion: male, female, villager, and warrior. Yes, I would like to lead that council, but I think the combined people of Eregion deserve a voice, and I will give it to them."

No more questions came. I finished my meal and moved to mount up. We rode until we came to the crossroads leading to the village where Kharis stole the babes from the mothers, and I hesitated for just a moment.

"Anyone wanting to shelter in the village, speak now," I asked, watching as several women rode forward. "Tralalis, you have the caravan; I'll secure their safety and catch up to you."

I didn't give her a chance to question. I kicked my mare into a gallop and wheeled away with a dozen women who would rather not fight at all. I understood them and felt no animosity at their decision.

We rode hard, cutting through the mountain passes at the fastest speeds possible. The thought lay in the back of my head that the warriors in the caravan could easily ambush me upon my return. It was a gamble telling them my plans ahead of time, but I meant what I said. They deserved to choose.

If they chose to fight me upon my return, I would fight. I understood from the beginning that not all the warriors disagreed with Kharis's social policies. There would be blowback. Just because you cut the head from the snake does not mean it will die immediately.

It took little time to reach the village. Our horses clattered into the square as curtains were pulled, and doors were barred. I understood this too.

"Faldwyn!" I shouted, turning my horse in a tight circle as villagers flew from their homes, axes and picks raised. "Faldwyn!" I yelled again, not wanting to draw my sword against these people.

"What is it Warrior, we have given all we can," she said, emerging from a nearby home, her face angry.

"Shelter these women, and I will die trying to return your babes to you," I said simply. "I plan to rule this land, but I need the help of everyone to make it the kind of place where people want to live. Do you understand? Time is short, and I have battles to wage," I said, hoping that she understood.

Nodding her head once, her face a mask, she took the reins of the nearest horse, and I whirled, galloping the way we came alone.

I caught the caravan as it entered the final stretch to the Capital City gates. The sun was low on the horizon, and we were still some distance away. The positive side of our delayed start was that Kharis would have expected us long ago. Since she never genuinely planned our return, our lateness might lull her into a false sense of security.

The downside was that we would arrive after dark. Snow had fallen while we were gone, and the reflected moonlight provided some light, but if a battle waged, and I hoped it would, the lack of light would have me at a disadvantage.

I circled the caravan from a distance, looking for anything amiss. The women rode alongside the wagons with Tralalis and Vonali in the rear. Maybe they did not believe I would challenge the Queen as no one had ridden ahead to warn her.

I trotted up behind the group, not wanting to trap myself by approaching from the front.

"They're tucked in," I said, pulling up alongside Tralalis.

"Good," she answered. "We follow you, Teagan," she said with no preamble. "All of us."

Vonali leveled me with her fierce gaze, and I met her stare. She nodded once and rode to the front of the line. We approached danger from the front with each passing step, so I left the flank to Tralalis and joined Vonali.

We came out of the last pass, and the gates spread out before us. The stark black and white beauty of the place caused my breath to catch. Despite the frigid chill and the ice, or maybe because of it, the place was lovely.

I kicked my horse into a slow canter, and the other women followed, leaving the wagons to a few. The gates swung open, and the townspeople stopped as we rode by.

The air was heavy with snow and a sense of quiet anticipation. In the silence, hooves echoed off the face of the palace, and I saw Kharis sweep onto her balcony, her Trio in tow. Clutching her arms to her chest, she fisted her hands, threw her head back, and screamed into the sky, showing the depth of her anger at my return.

"Kharis!" I screamed. "I challenge you for First Sword!" I infused my voice with magic so it would be heard for miles around.

Doors were barred, and shutters slammed as the people around us sought safety. Her eyes glittered as the moonlight reflected off the snow and struck them. I'm not sure how I ever thought her beautiful, for no soul lived behind those cold blue eyes.

"Take her!" she shouted, and warriors on horseback flowed like water around the buildings to intercept us. I raised my sword and held my mount still with my legs. Behind me, the sound of metal scraping against leather rang out, and I knew the time to decide had passed. We would win, or we would die.

From the far side of the palace, more riders approached at breakneck speed. Pameline and many other women fought their way to us. I watched as two sides of the same coin converged like a wave crashing into the shore: sister against sister, mother against daughter. I noticed then that many men rode as well, weapons raised. Their blood-curdling screams rang through the streets.

Kicking my mare, I raced into the fray with my sword held high and a warrior's scream on my lips. The women behind me followed, and we slammed into the wall of fighters with a flash of steel and grunt of bodies.

The warriors loyal to the Queen fought hard, but they were outnumbered and soon dropped their swords in surrender. The garrison that went to Tir fo Thuinn was not back, and that helped our side. They would come and find their lives had changed. They would adapt, or they would challenge me. I worried not, for I had already fought them all to claim Second Sword.

I searched the seething mass of bodies for my Trio, but there was no way to find them in the chaos. I fought my way toward the palace and Kharis. This battle would stop when her head hung from my hands.

"Kharis!" I challenged again, riding my horse to the doors of the palace. Jumping off, I entered the building in search of her.

In the halls, men fought other men with weapons and their hands. I walked past them, sword out, heading toward the main hall. I was met by four warriors intent on stopping me.

I raised my sword and engaged them, using magic and muscle to augment my speed. I raised my free arm and felt magic rush to my fingers. It was hard not to do a happy dance when a ball of fire flung from my hand, knocking the women down.

"Stay down. My fight is not with you," I said, sword in one hand and red ball of flames in the other.

"You will never rule here!" One jumped up, rushing me. I met her sword with mine and disarmed her in three strikes.

I flung the fireball at another group of warriors approaching me, and I realized that the Queen had kept her most loyal warriors to guard the halls. Letting out another yell, I cut through them with magic and Fae steel.

The blade of my weapon glowed bright red as I fought ten against one, then ten more. I blurred through them faster than they could register and killed those that refused to stand down. Magic augmented my every move, and my muscles flowed in ways I did not understand.

The warriors who did not die parted for me, dropping their swords and bowing their heads. I took off at a run, screaming for Kharis to show herself. My words echoed down empty halls and across vast open spaces. I crossed the throne room, my feet moving of their own accord.

I found her in the passage that led to the stables. Whether she thought to flee or join the fight, I did not know. They raced headlong on smooth stones with their swords out.

"Stop," I yelled, using magic to enforce the will of my words.

They froze, turning to face me with wild eyes and bared teeth. It was the first real emotion I ever saw her display. She spread her feet and dropped into a fighting stance, her sword out and silver hair flying around her face.

"You will die for this," she said, advancing on me. Her Trio spread around her with swords of their own drawn and bloodlust in their eyes as they tried to surround me.

Using magic, I placed a wall at my back that they could not penetrate. Screaming her fury, Kharis struck at me, and my sword glowed instantly red, shocking the men to momentary stillness. It didn't last, and all four came at me with a ferocity reserved for the self-righteous.

Using all my skill and magic, I fought, slashing and twirling away from their strikes. I flung a ball of magic at one of her men, dropping him where he stood. One of the others slashed at my shoulder, and my arm went numb. My magic fought to heal the wound but not quickly enough, and I stepped back, losing ground.

"You think you can best me, little girl?" She tossed her head back, laughing. I used her distraction to cut Hel'r down at the knees. She froze as his blood flowed across the stone path then came at me with everything she had. Our swords clashed in a frenzy of thrusts and parries.

I had always wanted to fight her, but she would not raise her sword to mine. She was skilled, very skilled. I was better, though, and she soon realized it. I pushed her back, causing her to stumble over Hel'r's body. Evar and Ronin circled behind me as I had let my wall drop. One of them slashed my hamstring with his sword, and I fought to keep my feet.

Pushing magic into my wounds and pulling more from the ground under the stones, I managed to stay upright.

Taking advantage of my momentary weakness, Kharis advanced with renewed frenzy, slashing and thrusting at me. I flung a fireball behind me, knocking her men back to protect myself.

For a moment, I thought it was over. I was injured, and though I was a better fighter than she, I was outnumbered, and her men were skilled swordsmen.

Using her size against her, I ducked under her reach and placed my back against the wall so that it was protected and fought with new vigor, but I was tiring despite the magic I pulled.

Thunder shook the palace, and the halls trembled from the power. The scent of ozone and wild things filled the air, mixing with spice and heather. Unbalanced, Evar stumbled, and I took his head, twirling back to face Kharis before she could take advantage of my turned back.

Her eyes narrowed in fury, and she screamed, jabbing wildly at me, all skill forgotten. I stepped into her over and over, pushing her back. I felt the last of her Trio move into my side, and I used the last of my magic to finish him. His body dropped, lifeless beside his brothers.

"It's over, Kharis. I am First Sword," I said, my chest heaving as I fought to catch my breath.

"Never!" she screamed, raising her weapon and rushing me. In one final strike, I took her sword and her head.

I slid down the wall, sinking into the blood of my enemies. Exhaustion overpowered me, and I closed my eyes.

It was over. I had no idea the extent of the damage, but it was done.

Leaning my head against the wall, I rested.

Chapter Twenty-Seven

Lyros

We cut our way through the crowds of confused warriors. Some raised their weapons against us, unsure if this was a slave uprising or a coup. Skirmishes erupted among the townspeople, and soon it was an all-out brawl.

I lost sight of Teagan in the melee as we fought the women loyal to Kharis with Pameline at our side. Shouts and screams added to the confusion. Riderless horses plowed through the streets, knocking over anyone in their paths. Small fires were set, and black smoke billowed into the square. My brothers and I fought slaves loyal to the warriors who were loyal to Kharis, and it was chaos.

I knew Teagan was in trouble but could not get to her. Each step toward the palace led to a new fight. It was like moving through frozen molasses- impossible.

Bodies lined the street, and I wondered if we would gain our freedom only to have nothing left. Black smoke changed to white, and heavy snow fell, obscuring our view.

My brothers and I fought our way closer to the palace, feeling Teagan's flagging strength in our souls.

Her desperation surrounded us, and we clashed with those in our way, putting metal on metal and fists on flesh to move closer to the entrance. Our swords glowed with Fae magic, and a path opened before us as others stepped aside in fear.

My magic triggered something, and a loud peal of thunder stunned the crowd to stillness. Kar moved the earth, and silence fell upon the square. Faces around me began to turn, and I followed their movement.

Dragging one leg behind her, a battered and bloodied Teagan appeared through the smoke and snow to stand on the balcony overlooking the fight.

"Enough," she said softly, infusing her voice with magic, causing the last of the fighting to cease.

Blood soaked and torn, the furred cloak she wore barely covered her arms. Her chest rose and fell heavily. Hair from her once tight braid blew around her in a tornado of curls. She swayed, tossing the head of the former Queen at our feet.

"I am First Sword," she said, pulling her blood-stained blade from beneath the furs to stand straight. She held it high, and it glowed softly red. "Any who wish to challenge me do so now or make peace."

On the balcony above us, she looked like what she was- a fierce warrior. Her eyes roamed the crowd, catching mine, and her sense of relief was evident, and when she caught sight of my brothers, a smile spread on her face.

"There has been enough death. Tonight, we mourn, but tomorrow we move forward. No more will men be crushed under the weight of Eregion Ice, and no longer will women have no choice in their mates, in their livelihood, and in their paths."

"As a people, we will grow and change together. Not one. Not ten. But the whole will be better for it. My Goddess reminds us that we are all her People, and under her guidance, we will prosper. Love who you will; find the path of your heart, and she will bring us peace."

"Never again will we rip babes from their mother's arms. Never again will we kill a man because his seed is potent. I am Eruhini," she shouted, raising her glowing sword to the skies. Lightning flashed down, striking it and setting fire to the tattoos that ran up her body. She arched her back as she was struck, and a hush fell over the crowd.

When the lightning ceased, she slumped, tilting her head back and rolling her shoulders. When she looked up, she was refreshed, and her eyes flashed with amber fire.

"I am Erhuhini, and we follow the Goddess. I am Erhuhini, and we are free. Tomorrow is a new day, and it will be what we make it."

Applause rang out in the square, first one hand, then many until cheers and roars boomed through the night. People hugged and danced in the streets, celebrating their new Queen.

In a flash, she was with us, her hands on our bodies and mouth crashing into ours. She pulled us to her, laughing and crying at the same time. One drum started and then another and, in the streets, people danced.

No one thought it would be easy, I'm sure of that, but the relief was palpable. Men grabbed warriors and spun them while they smiled.

Warriors and men alike moved to touch Teagan. They bowed at her feet, and her cheeks heated with embarrassment. She had not come to this land willingly, but willingly she had taken the mantle of leader and freed it. We were not the people of her blood, but we were the people of her heart.

In the days that followed, the dead were buried. Twenty-two warriors and thirty-seven men lost their lives and were mourned. The numbers were hard to swallow, but we would move on from the loss.

The villagers came forward to claim their young. The babes were returned immediately, but the older children stayed in the only homes they had ever known so they would not be traumatized again. Birth and adoptive parents worked together to ease their child's way into this new world.

A council was formed. Six men and Six women would make the laws, and as a People, we looked forward. Each village had representation and a voice in their future. As our Queen,

Teagan only voted if there was a tie to break. Complaints were heard, and disputes were settled using fairness, not force.

Markets sprang up, and commerce flourished. The long winter faded to the Eregion version of spring, and life was good. The opposite of change is stasis, and the land had been frozen in the past long enough. We did, indeed, move forward.

I watched her on her throne and knew there was no better place for her. Her bright red dress billowed around her legs, and she smiled, tapping her feet to the minstrels that played for us as the Luchorpán King danced with the next female. My brothers and I sit at her side, holding her hands and watching the joyous smile on her face.

Men wear long robes or tight pants below us, and women in dresses stretched tight over the bumps in their bellies dance with those men. In a few short months, Teagan's people know more peace and prosperity than they ever had under Kharis.

Magic abounded, and the Goddess showed herself often to her people. She also laughed with us, meeting us in the mirror when the pressure of our duties became too much. Sometimes we sneak away to swim in the lake and make love in the meadow. Lots and lots of love.

And we do love. All of us. From slavery to Kings, she raised us, yet there is nothing more magical than her pleasured sighs underneath our bodies. She is our gift from the Goddess- not the magic, not the elevation in our positions: Teagan.

The pens are emptied. Never again will a man or woman live like a beast in the bowels of this palace. Men choose men, women choose women, and they choose each other, but the bottom line is they choose. Matings are solidified, and bellies round in record time.

The Goddess blesses us all.

Epilogue

I come on Syl's thick cock when his silver bar piercing hits my Goddess Spot while Lyros works my mouth hard. My rounded belly gets in the way more now, but my appetite for these men is insatiable. Kar fears he will dent the baby's head and tries to be gentle. I laugh, pinning him with magic infused limbs and fuck him hard. Throwing my head back, I growl my pleasure and take his seed when he gives it.

Inside me, the baby they created moves in an irritated fashion. Maybe she is getting her head poked by those metal bars, or perhaps he's tired of the constant intrusions. Too bad. I love my men with a deep and abiding passion and can not get enough of them.

It doesn't matter if this baby has blue eyes or black- dark hair or light; it is ours, and we love him. Or her. My mates are deadly protective, and I know they will make amazing fathers.

This was not some magical babe born of all of them, but he was conceived in love and carried in peace.

My ankles swelled, and I look like a yak.

Our baby will have lots of company as maternity clothes are the new fighting leathers.

The people are happy, and it shows.

Does another war loom on the horizon? Yes, I know that it does. The Goddess said Ari's child was integral to that war, so we have time. Time to grow. Time to plan. Time to live. That my sister and I carry babes at the same time makes me smile. I just wish I could see her. Her ankles specifically. I want to know if they are as fat as mine.

When war comes, we will be ready, for we are still a nation of warrior men and women. We will not grow soft. My husbands and I will ride side by side, and the people of Eregion will help free the people of Talamh na Sithe. Maybe our child will ride with us, but that is their choice.

Lyros spills his sweet essence down my throat, taking my mind off war and fat ankles. I groan, swallowing all of him and trying to get more. He collapses under me with a laugh as another cock fills me.

Goddess, life is good.

My body stretches with another delicious orgasm, and I freeze as hot fluid seeds my already full womb, and the first pain takes me.

I shift, trying to get comfortable, but the next pain shuts me down. I moan and pant through it as molten liquid flows from my womb, and I know it's time.

Dani swore to me during my last pregnancy bitch session that the more I loved my men, the faster this kid would come.

She wasn't wrong.

My mates scramble away and run for the midwife.

Pameline comes rushing through the door with wide eyes and capable hands, and in half a day, we hold our beautiful son.

A son whose colors are a blend of Fire and Ice.

A son who, at birth, knows so much love that his parents cry just from looking at him.

A son who will never know the lash of a whip.

He is a child of Eregion and will always have a choice. And the world is a much better place because of it.

Hello!

I hope you enjoyed Teagan! Maybe now you understand why her story had to be told before the Healer Series's final installment, Goddess Bound, is released. I just love how Teagan developed, and I'm so glad she let me tell her story.

Please consider leaving a review! I love reading them, and they inspire me to do more and be better. Thanks again for taking the time to keep up with these characters.

Sharilyn

Sharilyn spent most of her early years on the Grand Strand of SC, annoying local police officers and probably pretty much everyone else. She graduated from the University of South Carolina and now lives on a small farm outside of Morgantown, WV, with various farm animals, her husband, and three kids who love to annoy her (Karma is a bitch.)

Sharilyn writes Urban Fantasy, Fairy Tales, and Omegaverse. She loves showing Quarter horses, trail riding, reading, and being annoyed by her kids. If she is missing, check for her horse trailer. If it is missing, no worries, she'll be back.

Healer Series:

Cerridwen's Tears

Healer

House of Fire

The Scarlet Heron

The Flame Keeper

Goddess Bound

The Eight Series:

Airmed

Ravena

Teagan

Omegas of the New South Series:

The Omega Rule

The Omega Challenge

An Alpha's Grace

Follow Sharilyn on Facebook, Instagram, Twitter, Goodreads, and her plain old website.

www.sharilynskye.com